THE
HAND
OF
THE
LION

Also by Carolyn Coker:

The Vines of Ferrara

The Other David

THE HAND OF THE LION

A Novel of Suspense

Carolyn Coker

DODD, MEAD & COMPANY New York

Published by Dodd, Mead & Company, Inc.,
71 Fifth Avenue, New York, N.Y. 10003
Manufactured in the United States of America
Production supervision by Mike Cantalupo
First Edition

1   2   3   4   5   6   7   8   9   10

Library of Congress Cataloging-in-Publication Data

Coker, Carolyn.
    The hand of the lion: a novel of suspense / by Carolyn Coker.—
1st ed.
        p.   cm.
    ISBN: 0-396-09191-1
    I. Title.
PS3553.O4367H3   1987
813'.54—dc19
                                            87-26343
                                            CIP

For Cal

Prologue:
Alexandria, Egypt (c. 83 A.D.)

"Leave his eyelids open."

The young sculptor who knelt beside the swathed corpse clenched his hands together to still their shaking. He looked up at the man with the gray beard who had spoken.

"Leave the eyes open," the older man repeated sternly, "and the mouth must stay as it is. Do not try to give him the appearance of a Roman statue."

The speaker turned quickly, moving off to join the small band of artisans preparing a makeshift furnace on the side of the hill. As he walked, the hem of his robe trailed a snakelike pattern in the sand.

The site where the men worked had been chosen carefully; its slight incline was enough to provide a view of the city to the east and the harbor to the north. All else was an endless sweep of desert. An intruder approaching from any direction could be identified long before he arrived.

Fading sunlight skipped and glinted on the surface of

the Mediterranean like a school of silver-bellied fish. Soon the daylight would be gone. That thought sent a chill through the young man beside the wrapped body and speeded him in his work. The prospect of touching the lifeless face when the sun no longer warmed it filled him with repulsion.

Reaching into the goatskin at his feet, he took a handful of moist clay. First flattening the carefully prepared earth between his palms, he pressed and stretched it beneath the chin, then up in front of and into the ears. The face had never been handsome. Now, framed in clay, it seemed grotesque with its staring lifeless eyes and the gaping mouth with its uneven upper lip.

The young sculptor's aesthetics tempted him to disobey the men who had hired him. By threading a needle-sharp sliver of a palm frond through the skin on the underside of the lips he could pull them together. And it would take no more than the touch of his thumb to mercifully close the eyelids.

"Continue as you were told." The older man had returned to check the artist's progress. Seeing the younger man hesitate, he added, "We must hurry. Leave the mouth as it is. He had no wish to be remembered for his beauty."

Hastily the sculptor continued to press clay onto the face with its distorted mouth and vacant eyes. He was afraid of the small band of fanatical men who had persuaded him to join them by paying a handsome fee in advance. But he was even more afraid of the Roman soldiers who would arrest, perhaps kill, all of them if they were discovered conducting burial rites that were against the laws of the Roman emperor.

To ease his tension, the sculptor tried to start a conversation with a nearby craftsman who was constructing a wooden coffin. "This man—was he your leader?"

"He was one of us," the other man answered without

looking up. Though obviously intent on his work and not willing to take time for a fuller explanation, he added, "In life he was a scribe."

That being so, the sculptor thought to take such risks was insane. And no one, he admitted to himself, was a greater fool than he for placing himself in such jeopardy merely for the payment of a few Roman coins.

As the men worked, the sky darkened as though smeared with charcoal. The pale lights of the city curved in a glowing crescent at the water's edge. From behind them the men could feel the first stirrings of a *khamsin*—a hot, dry wind from the Sahara. The wind speeded the drying of the clay and fanned the flames in the furnace where an ingot of bronze melted in a crucible.

When at last the mask was lifted off, the likeness of the face was transferred from clay to bronze. After the molten metal cooled, the sculptor had one last task: affixing the mask to wooden backing to give it extra strength. Then, after again swearing to secrecy, he was allowed to go.

As time passed, the secret of that strange assignment was like a stone that grew heavier the longer the young sculptor held it.

Many years later, when he had gained recognition throughout Egypt as an expert craftsman—having switched from sculpture to the more lucrative trade of making decorative metal fittings for ships—he told the story.

He no longer feared reprisal. The Romans were kept busy punishing present crimes and had scant interest in those of the past.

In the aging sculptor's favorite seaside tavern, he spoke often of that night on the hillside in Alexandria. Whether the story was believed or not, it crossed the sea with the sailors who heard it.

Still, the mask lay undisturbed in interment with the mummified body.

On the earth above the sepulcher, the Roman armies marched for half a millennium more until Moslem troops from Arabia captured Alexandria. Through the subsequent two hundred years of Moslem rule the sculptor's story survived.

At the beginning of the ninth century, an enterprising sea captain who had learned the location of the sepulcher arranged to steal the sealed coffin. He smuggled it out of Egypt beneath a load of pork, which he knew the Moslems would not investigate. The destination of the captain's ship was Venice.

There, in the city that called herself the Serenissima, the bronze mask survived fire and flood, but was never threatened by theft again until the eighteenth century.

In 1797, when Napoleon's army captured Venice, a young French captain made an attempt to claim the sculpture as a trophy of their victory. On his way out of the city, the officer carrying the mask in his knapsack was waylaid and nearly killed by an irate Italian citizen.

The French captain escaped with his life, but not his booty.

Like the Egyptian sculptor who told the story of the mask to the sailors in the tavern in Alexandria, Napoleon's officer had his own updated version. For many years the Frenchman repeated the narrative of the ancient bronze and how he almost smuggled it out of Italy. A few of his friends and family believed the story and retold it themselves.

Almost two hundred years later, one of the officer's descendants still believed it.

Chapter One

The new Obélisque apartment building was just north of the Champs Elysées and faced the Place de la Concorde. On the sidewalk in front were half a dozen pleasant chestnut trees and an ornate lamppost with three white globes set like giant pearls in wrought-iron prongs.

There were six floors above the lobby of the Obélisque, but inside the glassed-in elevator that skimmed the front of the building the numbered stops were one through five.

On a soft summer evening in late June, a suntanned man with striking white hair entered the empty elevator and punched an unmarked button. "Georges Tropard," he said into the small mesh speaker in the chrome control plate.

"Press the green button when you reach the top," a feeble voice instructed.

As the elevator ascended and the passenger's perspective widened, the half-dozen chestnut trees in front of the luxury apartment building became part of a countless number which stood straight and stately along the avenue that curved with the Seine. To the left were the Jardin des Tuileries and the Louvre; to the right were the Grand Palais and the Arc de Triomphe. And in the center, dominating the cloudless sky, was the Obelisk of Luxor; a four-sided shaft of stone that reached one hundred feet in the air and tapered to a pryrimidal point at the top.

The obelisk was a gift from Egypt to France at a time when the French were short of leaders to whom they could safely erect monuments. The original statue of Louis XV that had stood in the center of the Place de la Concorde had been knocked from its pedestal by an angry mob. A few years later, in the same city plaza, the head of Louis XVI had been lopped from his body by the guillotine. The ancient obelisk, it was decided, was not likely to cause controversy and so was erected as a symbol of peace. It was also the reason the owner of the Obélisque building leased the first five floors and kept the sixth for himself. He was a collector of antiquities and had searched for years for a suitable property where he could build a structure with an unobstructed view of the Egyptian marvel.

Georges Tropard pressed the green button and entered a room of floor-to-ceiling glass on three sides. The fourth wall was paneled oak and hung with portraits of five men, all painted in oils, and all in identical gold-leaf frames. They were the forebears of the apartment owner and arranged in sequence as revealed by brass plates with their names and dates. The most recent was of a somber, sharp-nosed gentleman in a dark business suit. The oldest painting was of a French army captain and bore the signature of Jacques Louis David, an artist who had numbered Napoleon among his clients.

The huge room was bare of furniture except for a grouping of two couches and three chairs around a rotating platform that held a large telescope. Spaced throughout the room and bathed in cones of light from concealed overhead fixtures were ten Plexiglas pedestals. Each of them supported an ancient Egyptian bronze statuette. A hippopotamus provided the model for one dated around 1800 B.C. Several were of cats, one was an exquisite representation of an Egyptian nobleman, in perfect condition except for one missing arm. The earliest dated from approximately 2000 B.C.; the most recent was of the first century.

Tropard had seen them all before, though not in their new setting. He had, in fact, acquired more than half of them for their owner. In some cases he had acted as the buyer's agent with a willing seller. At other times, when an object was not for sale, he had employed less public means of fulfilling his assignment.

"Georges, are you impressed with my new salon?" An elderly man in a wheelchair entered the room through a doorway in the oak-paneled wall.

"Yes, indeed," Tropard said. "It is perfection."

"Not quite. That's why I wanted to talk with you." The speaker maneuvered his wheelchair into an open space between the two couches. "But business can wait. First, sit down and take a look through this."

Tropard sat on the couch and adjusted the telescope as his host directed. Even to the naked eye the view of the obelisk in the Place de la Concorde was overwhelming. Magnified, the ageless hieroglyphics that climbed the stone shaft seemed as vital and clear as they must have appeared to those who gazed at them three thousand years ago in front of the temple of Luxor.

Tropard asked, "What do the hieroglyphics say?"

"They are a glorious account of the accomplishments of Ramses II," the man in the wheelchair said. With a small, dry laugh, he added, "Probably political lies."

Tropard smiled at his client. Then, he asked seriously, "Are you feeling well?"

"No. But I'll be around a while longer." The man straightened the cashmere lap robe. "You're looking fit, Georges." Then, in a tone that suggested that the amenities were over, he said, "Are you working on something at present?"

"Yes, I'm leaving in the morning for Florence. A collector with a fondness for Renaissance drawings has a lead on something he wants me to track down. He's had word that a sketch—a Ghirlandaio—is about to be smuggled out of the Italy. Naturally, a man with the sensibilities of my client does not approve of an Italian work of art being taken from its native land to America—which is the plan this would-be thief has in mind. My contact thinks that if the drawing is going to leave the country, at least it should not leave Europe. He is willing to keep it safe at his house on the Avenue Foch."

The two men laughed quietly. Then the man in the wheelchair said, "So you plan to go to Italy."

"Yes."

"Perfect. When you have finished in Florence, there is something you can bring back for me from Venice."

When the man in the wheelchair described the bronze sculpture he coveted—the one object that would make his collection complete—Tropard refused to take the assignment.

It would be impossible, he said. The sculpture was too well guarded, the risks were too great, a workable plan could take months to develop, and the cost would be prohibitive.

But even as he listened to himself recite the reasons why it could not be done, the thought of pulling off this most intricate of all the art thefts in his long career grew as an irresistible challenge.

When at last he stepped back into the glass elevator the

agreement had been made. And when he headed his black Porsche out of the parking garage beneath the Obélisque apartment building, he was already thinking of ways to shorten his stay in Florence and get on with the Venetian project.

Chapter Two

That year in July, the Maggio Musicale, the annual spring and summer music festival of Florence, concluded its season with performances by the visiting American Opera Company. The overall production was well received, but it was the superb tenor soloist who was responsible for the sellout crowds.

On closing night, Andrea Perkins sat second from the aisle in the garden amphitheater of the Pitti Palace. She had a rolled-up program in one hand and the fingers of her other hand were tightly laced in those of the Captain of Detectives of the Florentine Police Department, Aldo Balzani.

For Andrea, wearing formal green chiffon and Balmain perfume was a pleasant change from the turpentine-scented and paint-splattered jeans and shirts she usually wore each day in her work as an art restorer. Balzani was not in his usual garb of nondescript business suit, either.

"If you had your choice," Andrea whispered, "would you

rather be wearing your friend Leonard's *Pagliacci* costume or your rented tuxedo?"

"Who needs a costume? This tuxedo qualifies as a clown suit."

The applause had started.

It was the end of the first act and the chorus stepped forward to take a bow. The response of the audience ebbed and swelled as each of the soloists, in turn, took center stage alone: The most enthusiastic approval was given to Leonard Swanson, who was featured in the title role.

Andrea and Balzani rose to their feet with the rest of the audience urging Swanson back for one more bow.

"Leonard's not my friend. He's just a guy I knew in the opera club in college. Come on," he said, taking her arm, "I'll introduce you."

"Shouldn't we wait until the end?"

"No. He invited us backstage. He isn't on now."

The amphitheater was set against a natural background of cypress trees, ornamented with statues and tiered with marble. The garden setting, with the stage as the focal point, was the inspiration of Eleonora da Toledo, the First Lady of Florence in the mid-sixteenth century. Among the most positive contributions her husband, Cosimo I, made were to introduce the olive tree to Tuscany, to persuade the Florentine craftsmen to learn the art of tapestry-making, and to give Eleonora a free hand with the Boboli Gardens. She engaged the services of some of the greatest architects and designers of the day to create the most beautiful garden in Europe. They succeeded. Now, with the plantings long since matured, the ponds stocked with fish, and the fountains enriched with patina, the setting was perhaps even more magnificent than when the first audience gathered for an alfresco concert at the invitation of Eleonora and Cosimo de' Medici.

Andrea and Balzani hurried down an aisle, keeping their eyes averted from the indignant stares of patrons who found their mid-ovation exit an insult. Andrea linked her arm through Balzani's. The surprising chill of a sudden breeze and a feeling of dread made her shiver. Through the jacket of his rented tuxedo, she could feel the shape of Balzani's shoulder holster. She quickly drew her arm away. "Why do you need a gun at the opera?"

"I'm more or less on duty," he said casually. "But the gun's really just to impress Leonard."

"How? To show him what a tough critic you are?" She tried to laugh. "We're not going backstage just so the two of you can talk about the good old days in New Orleans, are we?"

Balzani's shrug was meant to be reassuring. "Leonard sounded nervous when he phoned to invite us. He said he was afraid of being robbed."

"Why? What makes him think that?"

"He's always been a little paranoid. At Tulane, he once accused a vocal coach—who happened to be Cajun—of putting a hex on him. He swore the man willed him to have laryngitis." Balzani put his arm around Andrea's waist. "If I thought there was a chance of real trouble, I wouldn't have brought you with me."

They were nearing the foot of the amphitheater where the aisle divided. On the right was the orchestra pit, on the left an intimate garden with a high hedge on three sides and a fountain with a statue of a frolicking water nymph in the center.

"He wanted me to send *several* of my best men to guard the stage doors tonight," Balzani said, "which should give you an idea of his opinion of his personal worth and that of his possessions."

"What is he afraid someone is going to steal?"

"He said he wasn't at liberty to explain." Balzani grinned. "I said *I* wasn't at liberty to assign detectives when there would already be a passel of crowd-control officers on duty."

"But you brought a gun anyway," Andrea said.

Balzani half-lifted her down an unlighted stone step at the corner of the hedge wall. "Just habit. You can't totally discount any complaint, even if it comes from someone like Leonard."

"And what about the extra men?"

"Extra man." Balzani nodded toward an indistinct figure in the shadows next to the stage door. "There he is."

The garden's shrubs and bushes acted as a buffer between them and the seats of the theater. From where they were, the splash of the fountain was louder than the sound of applause, and the crunch of their footsteps on the gravel path was distinct enough to make the other detective look quickly in their direction.

Balzani started to speak, but the man in the shadows held up a warning hand, then pointed sharply at the stage door. Balzani gripped Andrea's arm. They both stood motionless. "Stand behind the fountain," he whispered. "Stay there until I come back."

Uneasily, she obeyed. As she watched, Balzani inched toward the opposite side of the door, then flattened himself against the wall. There was almost no place to hide from the light of the full moon, which had chosen that moment to burn through a thin scrim of clouds.

There seemed to be no one else around. Andrea looked beyond the stage door to the road behind the amphitheater. Parked there, off the divided blacktop, was an empty van with Maggio Musicale written on the side. Next to the van were three deserted police cars. The men who had arrived in them were undoubtedly stationed among the crowd. At the head of the blacktop facing the wider paved thoroughfare was an ambulance—required by city ordinance to be at all large public functions. Andrea could now make out the driver and another white-uniformed man leaning against the side panel of the emergency vehicle. The coal of a cigarette moved up toward the mouth of one, then down at his side again.

The delivery area behind the stage looked empty from where Andrea stood. Then, slowly, a low sports car—it was identified later by the ambulance driver as a black Porsche—glided into view from the back of the building and stopped at the edge of the macadam apron that led onto the service road.

The car's headlights were turned off, and Andrea could not hear the sound of the engine above the splash of the fountain. She might not have noticed the automobile at all against the dark background, but the bright reflection of the moon on the high gloss of the hood and the way the light wavered as the car idled caught her eye. As she watched, a man emerged from the driver's side and stood, not moving, with the door still open.

She would never be sure of the exact sequence of events that took place in the next few seconds. She remembered distinctly that the detective assigned by Balzani stepped out of the shadows and into the light from the stage door. There was the sound of a gun. A woman screamed—

But before that. First. The stage door flew open, and a slightly built woman was silhouetted against the light from inside the buidling. The figure seemed to have no more dimension that a black cut-out hung in front of an unshaded light bulb. Even so, Andrea could tell that the person was hardly more than a girl. It was her hair, for one thing. She had masses of it. It curled above and around her head, and the light shone through at the edges in uneven glittery spirals. Her back was straight, her movements fast. And though she hesitated on the landing to get her bearings in the dark, she never really stopped. She took little dancing steps as she shifted her weight from one foot to the other, like a tennis player anticipating his opponent's serve.

She was clutching something to her chest—a large book or a package. Whatever it was, it blocked her view of the low stairs that led to the gravel path. Half turning, looking down over her shoulder, she moved sideways. It was then that Balzani's detective came forward, blocking her way.

The woman stiffened and stood motionless.

Balzani was poised to step forward onto the path.

A sudden movement near the sports car made Andrea look quickly in that direction. She saw the driver run toward the stage door. Something shiny in his hand glinted in the moonlight.

"Aldo! The parking lot! He has a gun!"

Aldo Balzani whirled in that direction. From the shadows he shouted, "Halt! You're covered!"

The man fired toward the sound of Balzani's voice.

The other detective, caught in the flood of light from the doorway like a player on an empty stage, lunged for the darkness and into the line of fire.

When the bullet entered the detective's back, the impact lifted him off the ground. His arms and legs spread apart, and for the split second he was in the air his face wore the horrified expression of someone being pushed over the edge of a precipice. He fell. But his fall was a short one—only the six inches between his feet and the ground, where he crumpled forward on his face.

The girl screamed, stumbled down the steps, and began running. The man with the gun grabbed her hand, pulling her behind him as they both ran so that she became his shield. Balzani never had a clear shot. There was never a moment when, if he had fired, he would not have hit the girl.

The gunman and his accomplice reached the black Porsche and were gone before anyone but Balzani and Andrea realized what had happened.

Chapter Three

The two attendants in white uniforms were amazingly fast and efficient, incredibly calm and accepting.

"There's a pulse," said one.

"He's breathing," the other pronounced.

The detective's arms and legs seemed to be connected with faulty hinges that allowed them to bend at peculiar angles when the men lifted him onto the stretcher. His eyes were unseeing. His brain, mercifully, had closed off the corridors of pain and thought. But the heart and lungs, like the two men who took their readings, continued to perform their function by rote.

The siren started only after the ambulance left the grounds, then blended with the sounds of the autostrada.

Ten, maybe fifteen minutes later—no, more like five, Andrea decided—she and Balzani were in Leonard Swanson's dressing room.

Neither the audience at the Maggio Musicale nor the performers were aware of what had happened outside the stage door. Still, to Andrea, the excited backstage laughter had a ghoulish ring, and the snatches of praise from cast members who followed Leonard Swanson to his dressing room sounded frivolous and inappropriate. "Best ever!" and "You were magnificent!" echoed down the hall.

The triumphant tenor left his admirers outside his door with suitably gracious words of thanks and turned to welcome his two invited guests.

"Aldo!" Swanson threw out his arms in greeting to Balzani and stood a moment holding the pose for effect.

He wore the traditional white satin costume of Leoncavallo's jealous clown, Canio, in *I Pagliacci*. His short neck was circled by a crinoline ruff. Fuzzy buttons that looked like giant black cotton balls started below his chin and progressed down past a beefy chest and bulging abdomen. His size ran to girth, not height. And as he stood in the doorway, there was a space of at least twelve inches between the pom-pom on the point of his cone-shaped hat and the top of the door frame.

His entrance did not receive the expected smile from either Aldo Balzani or Andrea. Undaunted, he kicked the door closed behind him, then with his leg still in the air, made a comic bow. "So this is the gallant captain's lady." Swanson rushed to take Andrea's hand and kissed it. "Without question, more beautiful than any painting she ever restored."

"Leonard," Balzani said sharply, "I need some answers from you. You're going to have to tell me now what you *didn't* tell me on the phone."

Swanson straightened and his own expression grew grim. His eyes darted to a steamer trunk in the corner of the room. It was open, and the combination lock hung uselessly from the hasp.

"Oh, my God!" The singer stepped backward and dropped heavily onto a chaise lounge. "Oh, my God, I've been robbed!" He braced his elbows on his plump knees and held his head in his hands. "Aldo, how could you have let someone do this to me?" As always, Leonard Swanson believed that the responsibility for any ill fortune that befell him rightfully belonged at someone else's doorstep.

Balzani left the wooden bench where he sat with a comforting arm around Andrea's shoulder. He looked down in disgust at the man in the clown costume, who seemed near tears over the loss of whatever had been in the trunk. In a moment, the captain of detectives pulled back the chair from the dressing table and straddled it, facing Swanson.

"I told you!" Swanson's voice quavered pathetically. "I told you this would happen!"

"I'll tell *you* what happened," Balzani said quietly through tight lips. "Then you tell me why."

Briefly and bluntly Captain Balzani described the earlier scene outside the theater that ended in the shooting of the Florentine detective. "Now, who was the man in the Porsche, and who was the girl?"

"I don't know." Swanson looked slightly chastened.

"Tell me what you know, Leonard. Tell me what it's all about." Balzani's hands tightened on the back of the chair as he leaned forward. "Who were they, and what did they steal?"

"Truly, I don't know who they were."

Balzani stood and crossed to the door, leaning against it. "*I* can live without the final scene of *Pagliacci*," he said, crossing his arms and planting his feet, "but the audience might get restless. You're not leaving this dressing room until you tell me."

It may have been the memory of seeing Aldo Balzani as a menacing presence in his football uniform at Tulane or perhaps a genuine concern for the paying customers of the Maggio Musicale; whichever, Leonard Swanson began to explain what he knew of the theft.

"It didn't even belong to me. It was a Ghirlandaio pen-and-bister."

"A what?"

"A pen-and-bister. It probably dated back to the late fifteenth century."

"A drawing." Andrea spoke for the first time since Swanson entered the room. "A preliminary sketch artists usually make before they actually start a major painting or fresco. Ghirlandaio sometimes used chalk on paper, sometimes a pen-and-bister."

"Like pen-and-ink?"

"It's the same sort of thing. Bister is a brown pigment made from soot."

"And a drawing like that from the fifteenth century would be valuable." Balzani did not actually make it a question but looked to Andrea for confirmation.

"If it were done by Ghirlandaio, yes."

"Yes," Swanson echoed.

"If it didn't belong to you, Leonard," Balzani turned back toward the tenor, "why did you have it here in your trunk?"

There was a knock on the door. A voice filtered through. "Ten minutes till curtain, Mr. Swanson."

Leonard Swanson looked anxiously toward the door, willing the police detective to one side, but Balzani did not move. Then, with a nervous sigh, convinced that there was no other way to get rid of his former colleague but to give an explanation, he began.

"The American Opera Company is hardly a profit-making organization. We have to depend on wealthy benefactors to sustain us. So we court them. We consider their preferences when we make out our yearly schedule of productions. We take their suggestions as to sets and costumes, we accept their recommendations of contractors to build the sets, printers to design the programs . . . you get the idea. We need their money, so we aim to please."

Swanson stood and adjusted his clown's hat in the mirror, then turned back to Balzani. "As it happens," he continued, "our number-one philanthropist is a collector of Italian Renaissance drawings. When he found out that we were scheduled for this appearance in Florence, he invited me to dinner one evening to present me with his plan. Actually, he's the one who arranged our schedule. It was through his connections that we were invited to perform at the Maggio Musicale."

Absently, Swanson had rubbed the side of his face as he spoke. He looked down now at his hand in dismay. It was covered with *clownwhite* makeup. "Oh, God! Now I'm going to have to have my face redone before I go back on stage," he said in a pleading tone.

"The faster you finish your story, the faster we'll leave," Balzani said.

"As I told you, it was our munificent benefactor who arranged our European schedule to include Florence. And though I hate to admit it, I don't think his number one reason was so the Italian operagoers could hear my *Pagliacci*, but so that I could act as a courier to bring back that damned drawing he bought."

"Wait a minute," Balzani said. "What's the matter with Federal Express?"

"My dear Aldo! Do you have any idea how rare that pen-and-bister is?"

"Yes, I've got some idea. But I don't see what makes you the ideal delivery boy."

"He trusts me." Swanson sounded genuinely offended.

Balzani laughed. "Who was the seller? Was it privately owned?"

"Oh, yes! It was delivered to me by the owner this afternoon."

"If your guy could afford to buy it in the first place, surely he wasn't going to try to sneak it out of the country just to avoid going through customs . . ."

"I think that must be exactly what he had in mind," Andrea said.

Both men turned and looked at her questioningly.

"It's illegal to take a work of art that old out of the country. And I think there was a second problem, wasn't there, Mr. Swanson?"

The tenor did not answer. He seemed to be studying the tassels on the toes of his clown shoes.

"What do you mean?" It was Balzani who asked the question. Swanson obviously did not want to discuss it.

"I think I know which drawing it was," Andrea said. "It was a detailed sketch for the *Adoration of the Shepherds*, wasn't it?"

"I barely looked at it," Swanson said as though addressing a minor point. "I just wanted to get back home and be rid of it."

"I heard at the office that a Ghirlandaio pen-and-bister had been stolen," Andrea said. "It was the big news around the water cooler a few months ago." Andrea's office was at the Galleria dell' Accademia in Florence where she was "acting" assistant curator. "Acting," only because to accept the title officially would mean a commitment to stay in Italy. She was not sure she could tie herself to something—or someone, for that matter—so far away from Boston.

"What do you mean a couple of months ago?" Still blocking the doorway, Balzani temporarily ignored Swanson and turned to Andrea for information.

"If it's the same one, it was a famous pen-and-bister drawing that had been owned for generations by a family in Siena. It's famous, at least, among people who are interested in Italian Renaissance art. Over the years, there had been any number of offers from collectors who wanted to buy the sketch, but the family had always refused. Then, last spring it was stolen."

"I see," Balzani said. "So the drawing was *already* stolen property when it was stolen from you, wasn't it, Leonard?"

"Let's just say I won't be filing a complaint."

Balzani's tone was more threatening than before. "A man was shot tonight—for all I know, he may be dead—because of some stupid idea of smuggling a picture out of the country. Now. How were you going to do it, Leonard? Tell me that. Whatever that girl carried out of here was larger than a single sheet of drawing paper. What was it?"

Swanson pointed to the trunk. "That's where we keep the musical scores for the orchestra, the chorus, and the soloists. It has a double lock, and it's fireproof. Our illustrious patron of the American Opera Company had my libretto especially bound in a volume with pages the same size as the drawing. The back endpaper had a flap that opened like an envelope . . ."

"And if by chance you were questioned either leaving Italy or entering the United States, I'm sure you would have had no knowledge of how it got there."

Swanson nodded without raising his eyes to Balzani's face.

"But how did you know someone was going to try to steal it from *you*?"

"The gentleman of my acquaintance is not the only wealthy collector of Italian Renaissance art. Among his rivals, he told me, is a man in Paris who also wanted this particular pen-and-bister."

"What's his name?"

"I swear to God, Aldo, I don't know."

There was another knock at the door. "Two minutes, Mr. Swanson!"

"My makeup!" The tenor soloist jumped to his feet. "You've got to let me get the makeup girl in here. I can't do the second act with my face smudged this way."

Balzani stepped aside and opened the door.

"Francesca!" Swanson ran into the hall calling for the makeup mistress. "Makeup! Francesca! Does anybody know where that cursed girl is?"

Nobody did.

Chapter Four

The black Porsche headed north through Bologna and Ferrara toward Venice. It averaged an easy seventy miles per hour until it reached Mestre, where it left the Autostrada del Sole and shunted onto a causeway across a shallow salt lagoon. At the end of the causeway, the signs directing incoming traffic pointed in only one direction: to the Piazzale Roma— a giant parking lot.

A motorist whose destination was Venice had no choice but to leave his car here; he would have no further use for it in the floating city.

It was well past midnight when the Porsche entered the gates of the parking lot. The driver said needlessly to the makeup girl from the Maggio Musicale, "We're here."

There was no other moving vehicles that late at night, but the smell of exhaust fumes and diesel fuel hung heavy in the still air. Row upon row of dark and silent tour buses, motor coaches, vans, trucks, and cars seemed to stretch for acres.

There were several empty parking spaces, but the driver of the Porsche had no thought of leaving his expensive automobile outside where it would be exposed to the elements, and possibly to the view of someone who had seen it leave the Boboli Gardens in Florence. He drove directly to the seven-story parking garage that dominated the piazza.

A sharp blast of the sportscar's horn woke the dozing attendant. A few minutes later, having been persuaded by of a handful of lire, he directed the driver to a well-protected parking space in a corner on the top floor.

There were only two pieces of luggage to unload: the girl's small, shabby suitcase and the man's pigskin overnighter.

After locking the *I Pagliacci* libretto with the concealed drawing in the trunk, the driver and the girl adjusted a canvas cover over the Porsche and left the garage.

Opposite the deserted sidewalk, they boarded a water taxi that took them to the private dock of the Hotel Mediterraneo.

At the reservation desk in the lobby, the man identified himself to the uniformed desk clerk. "Tropard, Georges Tropard." Tropard's manner was that of someone who is accustomed to receiving immediate attention.

The reservation book was quickly opened on the polished mahogany desk, and as the clerk hurried to locate Tropard's name, the bell captain—the only other person in the elegant lobby—took charge of the two pieces of luggage.

The girl stood waiting by the elevator. And though hotel policy allowed the bell captain only a discreet glance in her direction, he noticed her unkempt hair and that her large brown eyes were red-rimmed as though she had been asleep—or crying.

"Ah, yes, Monsieur Tropard. We've been expecting you," the desk clerk said, looking up from the page where his finger marked a line that read: "Tropard, Georges—Paris—

Businessman." The arrival time was noted as late Wednesday or early Thursday. Suite 326 had been reserved and was paid in advance for one week, and beneath the date of departure was written "*Indefinite.*"

After the bell captain led Tropard and the girl to their suite and returned to the lobby, he and the desk clerk looked at each other and shrugged. It was as though their personal appraisal was the final phase of guest registration.

"His daughter, would you say?" The desk clerk always made the same smirking comment when there was such an obvious disparity in age as that between Tropard and the makeup girl.

The bell captain grinned. "Or perhaps his niece."

With a sigh—not of censure but of envy—the desk clerk glanced at the reservations log to make sure no other late arrivals were expected, then slid the book back onto the shelf beneath the desktop. The bell captain yawned and headed for an ormolu chair behind a large brass planter to resume his nap.

The next morning, Georges Tropard took the makeup girl, Francesca Pellegrino, shopping. This fulfilled a promise he had made when she agreed to help him steal the Ghirlandaio drawing. He also had promised to take her to Paris when he completed the project that had brought them to Venice.

At the time he mentioned Paris, he had even thought he *might* take her back with him. But her tears and lamentations about the man Tropard had shot in Florence were becoming a bore. Still, for the time being, Tropard needed Francesca's help.

On the following day, *Il Gazzettino* carried a brief account of the backstage robbery at the Maggio Musicale. Leonard Swanson was not named as the victim, nor was the Ghirlandaio drawing mentioned. It was reported, however, that a Florentine detective had been shot and was rushed to the

Hospital of Santa Maria Nuova where he had undergone surgery.

"You see? He is not dead." Tropard pointed out the article to Francesca, who was still in bed when he came back from the newstand in the lobby. "He'll survive," Tropard said, taking her hand in his and kissing the palm.

Francesca smiled for the first time since they left Florence. This was the Georges who had made her melt like *gelato*, not the one who had fired the gun without hesitating. *Her* Georges had taken her for long drives in his Porsche telling her of Paris; asking her questions about herself and her job at the Maggio Musicale. He had not even tried to make love to her the first time they met. It was only after they had many long talks together that he asked her to come to his hotel room. When she agreed, and they entered the lobby, he held her hand so gently that she could have left at any time. That was why she went with him.

"He'll be as good as new. Those doctors know what they're doing. Removing one small bullet is not such a dangerous thing."

Francesca chose to believe him. It was the way she always dealt with her conscience. It would have been different if the man had died—death was difficult to ignore. She had never been able to rationalize death. When she was a schoolgirl she had lost her faith in the stories the nuns told of a more glorious life to follow. If that had been true, then why would death be so ugly and why, at the end, had Francesca's mother been too weak to lift her head from the pillow but still strong enough to scream in pain? And her younger brother who had drowned; had he gone to a better place in that blue and bloated body they had dredged from the Arno? Where was the golden light? Where was the beautiful Christ in the spotless white robe with the outstretched hands?

The look of terror in the eyes of the detective when

Tropard shot him had almost paralyzed Francesca with fear. But he was still alive! The newspaper said so. He had escaped whatever it was he had seen of death. He was being cared for at Santa Maria Nuova, where there were fine surgeons, clean sheets, solicitous nurses, and vases of flowers.

In a short time, Francesca was happily considering which of the new dresses she should wear that day.

For Venice, it was still early in the morning when Tropard and Francesca left the hotel and walked the short distance to St. Mark's Square. The hands on the Clock Tower's zodiac timepiece were on the Aries and the Pisces—ten to nine. Most of the small tables and chairs in front of the sunny cafés were still vacant.

Waiters in morning-fresh white jackets stood chatting in groups of threes and fours. On the open-air bandstand, a piano player unlocked the keyboard while other musicians on the day shift of the tireless orchestra opened instrument cases, the bass player resined his bow, and the drummer practiced paradiddles on the snare drum.

As Tropard and Francesca crossed between two arches of the covered walkway, a veteran waiter in front of Quadri watched them approach his section of tables.

Francesca paused a moment in the sunlight, looking quickly in each direction, uncertain which way to turn. With a tight smile, Tropard spoke softly to her. Then with his hand lightly at her waist, he guided her through the closely packed chairs to a table at the far end of the café under an awning.

Tropard had the kind of good looks some men attain only with middle age. For him, it was a matter of the change in the color of his hair and the interesting slanted furrows in his forehead that had developed from his habit of cocking a skeptical brow at the world. Until he was in his early forties, his hair had been a nondescript sandy shade. But for the past ten years it had been white, not streaked, or silver, or gray, but

31

stark white. And with the tan he carefully maintained year round with a sunlamp, and with the silk scarf he wore instead of a tie, one could imagine that he spent his evenings in private, genteel card games for high stakes and his days at the helm of a sleek racing yacht that he had designed himself.

At least that was the assessment of the waiter who took Tropard's order for coffee.

It was not surprising to see a man of this type with a girl less than half his age. It was to be expected, the waiter thought. But not this particular girl.

She was pretty enough. Her hair was lustrous and black, as were her eyes. But her clothes, though obviously new, seemed too sophisticated for her. The low neckline of the loose bodice was designed to show a hint of cleavage. But she kept clutching at the soft pastel fabric as if in embarrassment, pulling it up toward her shoulder, which threw the whole effect off center.

One would expect, the waiter thought, that a man such as this would have chosen a girl like one of the fashion models who were often photographed against the background of Venice for magazine advertisements.

"Signore, perhaps you and the signorina would care to move to a table nearer the front if you have come to see the pigeons being fed." The waiter spoke in Italian, confident that it was the girl's native language, but wondering if the man were French.

"No. This is the table I want," Tropard replied in Italian with a thick French accent. "You'll be comfortable here, won't you, Francesca?"

Francesca smiled at Tropard, and her look of innocent acceptance roused the same protective instinct in the waiter that he felt for his own daughters. This girl would have agreed, he thought, if the Frenchman had said, you're going to climb to the top of the Bell Tower and jump off, arent' you, Francesca?

"We'll have only coffee," Tropard said in dismissal. "And we would like it—now."

With a curt nod and dark thoughts about the predatory ways of some men, the waiter wordlessly served them and left to ready the nearby tables for a group of twenty-five or so tourists he saw heading toward the café.

Pigeons flew out of the path of the new arrivals who crossed the square. The group was led by a young man holding aloft a closed red, white, and blue umbrella. The umbrella was a prearranged rallying point, a sort of combination captain's flag to keep the troops from scattering and a glimpse of home for the benefit of tour members who wandered away and had trouble finding their fellows again.

As always with a group, there was a polite contest for the best seats. When all the tables in Quadri's roped-off section were filled, there were still three teen-age girls left standing.

The girls—all in shorts and tank tops—had waited until everyone was seated, but not out of excessive politeness: rather by design. Whenever possible, they tried to get special attention from the handsome young tour director.

At the moment, he was assisting the waiter in getting two retired schoolteachers settled with their jackets, cameras, and one plastic shopping bag each that contained extra shoes, wrapped sandwiches, and guidebooks.

"I'll take care of you girls in just a moment," the director said, raising his eyebrows in an imitation of a Groucho Marx leer.

The girls giggled. The schoolteachers smiled knowingly, indulging vicariously in the flirtation. The director had, after all, seen to their needs first.

Though this summer was Kyle Hagen's first as a tour

director, he did his job well. He quickly learned the special attentions each of his charges required to stay interested and happy.

"We'll need three more chairs," he said in Italian to the waiter. "There are twenty-seven in the group. Bring them all coffee and sweet rolls, and the bill is to go to Global Tours at the Hamilton Plaza Hotel."

"Yes, sir." The waiter made a note on his order pad. "And your name sir?"

"Hagen, Kyle Hagen," he said quickly, taking hold of the waiter's sleeve to keep him there a moment.

"Reverend Thompson!" Hagen held the umbrella up to get the group's attention. This was going to be a corny routine, Hagen thought, but what the hell. It might be worth a laugh. The man whose name he had called answered.

"I want you to hear this," Hagen said to the bald Baptist minister in a madras shirt. "I told the waiter we'd need three more chairs. And *he* said . . ." Turning toward the waiter, Hagen prompted good-naturedly, "Say your line again."

"*Scusi?*" The waiter had no idea what the tour director meant.

"Say it again. What you just asked me."

"Your name? What is your name?"

"Right!" Hagen let go of the waiter's sleeve, and in the manner of an orator, said, " '*And he asked him, What is thy name? And he answered, saying, My name is Legion.*' " Pointing to the minister to finish the quotation, Hagen said. "And the reason we need more chairs, *is* . . ."

" '. . . *for we are many.*' " The minister found it difficult to smile, but could not resist adding, "The Book of Mark, chapter five, verse nine."

The group laughed.

Reverend Thompson continued. "Mark, of course, was talking about a legion of unclean spirits . . ."

"No preaching, dear," interrupted the minister's wife, who wore a blouse of the same madras print as her husband's shirt. "We're on vacation."

Within minutes the waiter was so busy serving the Global Tours group that he had no time to puzzle over the encounter with the Scripture-quoting tour director. Nor did he give any further thought to Tropard and Francesca until he happened to glance in their direction. What he saw confirmed his first impression that the Frenchman was rude and inconsiderate. He had turned his back to his companion and seemed interested only in studying the private stairway next to his table. With a pretty young girl seated beside him, what could be so fascinating about the entrance to the office of the Society for the Preservation of Venetian Art?

"*Subito! Subito!*" The waiter snapped his fingers, then pointed out the next table to be served by a busboy who carried a metal tray with a dozen cups and a large pot of coffee. Seeing that done, the waiter hurried into the kitchen for the baskets of sweet rolls.

Tropard sat with a leather-bound notebook that fit in his palm and a gold retractable pen. At nine-ten, he made the note: *Older woman (secretary?) unlocked door at the head of the stairs and entered.*

Nine-twenty: *Mario Costantino arrived.*

It had been some time since he had seen the Director of the Society for the Preservation of Venetian Art, but he recognized Costantino. They had met at Connie Gilbert's villa in Venice when Tropard had delivered a sketchy Manet watercolor to Mrs. Gilbert, an avid collector of French Impressionist paintings.

Tropard was confident that Costantino had not seen

him seated at the table in front of Quadri. Good. It was not yet time to renew the acquaintance.

Nine twenty-five: *Man in charge of American tourists entered Costantino's office.*

The visit, Tropard supposed, was related to a tour of the Basilica or a museum. But the American had seemed, somehow, furtive. He had stopped at the foot of the stairs and looked back, as though hoping no one in his group had seen him slip away. His behavior was worth a question mark in Tropard's notebook.

Nine-thirty: *American tour director returned. He seemed distraught. No, angry! Quite angry. Why?*

Chapter Five

In the second-story office overlooking St. Mark's Square, Mario Costantino's secretary stood with one hand on the knob of the partially open door between the reception room and the inner office. With her other hand she smoothed a loose strand of graying hair away from her round, unsmiling face. "That American, Kyle Hagen, was here again," she said.

"Yes, I heard. It's a nuisance, I know, but perhaps he'll soon get tired of stopping by." Costantino gave his secretary a sympathetic smile.

The woman in the doorway shrugged. Her theory was that the only questions that needed answers were those that concerned the mechanics of running the office, not the intrigue. Her original instructions were that if Kyle Hagen telephoned, Signor Costantino was not in. If he came to the office, Signor Costantino was too busy to see him. Apparently that had not changed. She closed the door between the two offices and went back to her typewriter.

Mario Costantino briefly stared at the space his secretary had filled, wishing Kyle Hagen would vanish as easily behind a closed door. Hagen's persistence was a problem he would have to solve, but for the moment he had been granted a reprieve. Gratefully, he turned his attention back to the letter he had been drafting to Andrea Perkins.

> . . . delighted that you will be joining me on the restoration project at the Basilica.
>
> I feel a measure of disappointment that you will not be available sooner, however, considering the large number of tourists in Venice during the last two months of summer, October probably is a better choice. By then, there will be only a few small guided tours through the cathedral each day, and you can set up your equipment and attend to your work undisturbed.

The last paragraph touched on details of the project that Costantino wrote could be more specifically outlined later.

Next to Andrea's name he scribbled, "Galleria dell' Accademia—Florence," and put the letter on the edge of his desk where his secretary would find it before the day was over.

That finished, the thought of Kyle Hagen returned.

It was possible, Costantino told himself, that he was worrying about nothing. A check for a few thousand lire might settle the whole thing. But it was possible that Hagen would consider it an insult to be offered money. Or—and this was the thought that stood Costantino on his feet and sent him pacing to the open window—perhaps one check would be only the beginning.

A fat pigeon landed on the balustrade and strutted back and forth in front of the sill as though patroling the area. Mario Costantino gave the pigeon a nudge that sent it flapping down to join the hundreds of others that flocked around the square. The disgruntled bird landed on the plastic shopping bag that belonged to one of the retired schoolteachers, then hopped to the stone floor of the square and pecked at the crumbs of a sweet roll at her feet.

If the former English literature teacher had glanced up and seen Mario Costantino framed in the arched window of the white building with its Byzantine façade, she might have been reminded of Lord Byron or Robert Browning, both of whom had lived and worked in Venice. It would be easy to imagine that Byron had stood in that room looking across at the symbol of Venice, the winged lion on its granite pedestal, as he composed a stanza of *Don Juan*. Or that Browning, while mourning his Elizabeth, had gazed solemnly at the square from that very window.

Romantic as the picture was, the purpose of the building then, as now, was to provide space for conducting the business of the city. Still, as Mario Costantino leaned against the window in his office, there was something about him that would put one in mind of a poet. It might have been the vulnerable slope of the shoulders, or the dark hair that fell across his forehead and shaded his eyes. At least that is how he would have appeared from the distance of one of the tables in front of Quadri's.

Closer up, it would not be difficult to guess Costantino's age correctly as late forties. His face, though still handsome, had lines around the mouth and at the corners of his eyes. And the furrows between his brows would be even deeper tomorrow because of his worried expression today. But the eyes still held a hint of poetic sensuality that was affirmed by the way he used his hands. As now, his fingers did not merely rest on the edge of the windowsill, they moved softly as though testing the roughness of the wood where the paint was chipped away. In a handshake, he was always conscious of the texture of the skin of the offered hand, of its warmth or coolness and of whether it was moist or dry. In his clothes, the feel of the fabric was more important than the fit. It gave him pleasure to run his hand across the sleeve of a silk shirt or down the leg of soft wool trousers. His tactile sensitivity had led, in younger days, to his expressing his emotions with a paint brush rather than in verse. And his aspirations as an artist had led, in turn, to his long relationship with Connie Gilbert.

For twenty-five years he had been the lover of the wealthy American. He was not the only one, but was the most enduring. And the present problem of Kyle Hagen was as much Connie's concern as his.

Hagen had said the first time he telephoned that he had tried to reach Mrs. Gilbert but had been referred to Mario Costantino instead.

Turning away from the window, Mario crossed to the desk and opened the middle drawer, where he kept his personal checkbook. Strange, he thought, how his and Connie's situations had reversed. At the beginning, she had been in charge; she had made all the decisions. When he still believed that success as an artist had everything to do with desire and that talent was something one could will into being, Connie had believed it, too. She, the mature romantic, had offered the young Mario her patronage and her bed. He had accepted both with pleasure. Now, long after his dreams and Connie Gilbert's husband were dead, a bond remained between them. It was to be expected that Connie would refer Kyle Hagen's telephone call to him.

Mario scrawled his signature at the bottom of a check for one thousand American dollars, payable to Kyle Hagen.

Taking a sheet of plain typing paper he wrote:

I'm sorry I was unable to see you when you called at the office this morning. It is understandable that you are disappointed at not being able to talk with Mrs. Gilbert personally. She regrets that her health is such that she sees very few visitors these days.

Please know, however, that she does appreciate your expression of sympathy at the loss of her daughter. Your friendship to Sandra while she was in California, especially at the last, must have meant a great deal to a young woman in her distressed emotional state.

Mrs. Gilbert thought it was possible that you had suffered some financial as well as personal loss because of Sandra's death, so please accept the enclosed check in the spirit in which it is given.

Sincerely,
Mario Costantino

Folding the sheet of paper, Mario stuffed it with the check into a plain envelope, which he hastily addressed. He instructed his secretary to call a courier service and have the letter delivered to Hagen's hotel.

"And if he calls again?"

"Continue as before," Mario replied to the secretary, "tell him I'm not in."

A week later, the check for one thousand dollars was returned with a note from Kyle Hagen expressing his thanks. The note stated that all Kyle wanted was a few minutes of Mrs. Gilbert's time to tell her of Sandra's brief return to consciousness before her death. Also, for the first time, Hagen made a reference to Sandra's daughter—Connie Gilbert's granddaughter. He even knew the child's name. Mary Louise—he wrote—was much on Sandra's mind at the last.

Mario, with greater resolve than before, wrote back, stressing Connie Gilbert's state of health. He suggested that it was difficult enough to overcome her grief—as perhaps it was for Kyle Hagen, too—and that it would serve no useful purpose to dredge up the past.

Before the end of August, Kyle Hagen stopped twice at the office of the International Committee for the Preservation of Venetian Art and was told both times that the chairman was out of the city. Once Hagen called in person at Connie Gilbert's villa and was refused admittance.

Early in September, Mario Costantino received a note saying that Kyle Hagen's original intent had been merely to console Mrs. Gilbert, but if she was unable to receive him, he had information which he was sure Mario would find interesting, and he vowed to hold it in confidence. Mrs. Gilbert need not be involved at all, he said.

There was no reply.

And that was the end of it. There were no more telephone calls from Kyle Hagen, no more notes, no more unscheduled visits to Costantino's office, no more attempts to see Connie Gilbert.

Mario Costantino was much relieved, but still wary. He had not expected that Kyle Hagen would give up without some sort of confrontation. At first he thought perhaps Hagen had left Venice. But he had seen him on several occasions with his red, white, and blue umbrella, leading a changing group of tourists around St. Mark's Square and into the Basilica. Whatever had brought about the change, Costantino was grateful.

He had no reason to be. What had brought about the change was the Kyle Hagen had become acquainted with Georges Tropard.

Chapter Six

At first, Kyle Hagen thought Georges Tropard was a private detective. Very often, after one of Hagen's unsuccessful attempts to see Mario Costantino, he would notice the man with the silk scarf and the suntan watching him when he left the office. The man was usually seated at the same table in St. Mark's Square. Sometimes he was alone; sometimes a pretty young girl with unkempt dark hair was with him.

If he was a detective, Hagen thought, he was not very subtle. Occasionally, the man even made notes in a small leather notebook.

It was becoming annoying. What the hell, Hagen had not done anything illegal, he told himself with the righteous indignation of someone was has been unsuccessful in carrying out a less than honorable plan. He decided to confront the man who had been keeping track of his visits to the office of the Committee for the Preservation of Venetian Art.

That particular day, Tropard was alone. When Hagen approached the table, the older man stood and smiled, as though he had been expecting the young tour director and was willing to forgive him for being late.

"Ah, Monsieur Hagen! I am Georges Tropard." The Frenchman reached into his pocket for the small notebook and hastily scribbled something on one of the pages. "I think we have matters to discuss that will be of great benefit to both of us." He capped his gold fountain pen and returned it to the breast pocket of his Pierre Cardin jacket. "I am staying at the Mediterraneo Hotel, the address is here." He tore a page out of the notebook and handed it to Hagen. "This evening at nine would be convenient, if that is agreeable with you." Tropard turned to leave.

"Just a minute! What's this about?"

"No, no. This is no place to talk. We should meet in the salon at the Mediterraneo about nine. I think you will find our conversation interesting—unless you have better things to do." He smiled, then began to walk away. "I will count on seeing you then," he said, almost over his shoulder.

Hagen did not answer, but he kept the appointment.

In the Mediterraneo Salon, Tropard had the home field advantage. He was well acquainted with the wine list and the personnel, while Hagen was a stranger there. And Tropard's light blue dinner jacket was worth a number of points over Hagen's worn corduroy sport coat. Still, Hagen was determined to play it cagey. He volunteered only that he had tried to see Mrs. Gilbert and that Mario Costantino stood in the way.

Let the Frenchman assume, if he wanted to, that Hagen was a drifter who was trying to ingratiate himself with the wealthy American widow. That was truly all it was—at first.

"Since you have had no success alone, would it not be expedient if we worked together?" Tropard looked companionably at his guest over the rim of his glass with the etched initial of the hotel.

"So, what you're asking me to do," Kyle Hagen said, feeling warmed by the brandy and more confident of his footing, "is to cast down my nets and follow you." Biblical allusions came easily and often to Hagen. He had made quotations from the Book of Mark part of his monologue when he conducted tour groups through St. Mark's Basilica. "You want us to join forces to become *fishers of men*."

"Not *fishers of men*, my friend; one man only." Tropard motioned for the waiter to refill their glasses. "Mario Costantino is the man we both want to catch."

"I can't see how it would be to my advantage," Hagen said.

Tropard signed his room number to the check the waiter handed him and asked that the bottle of cognac be left on the table between the two men.

"You wish to meet with Madame Gilbert," Tropard said when the waiter was gone.

Hagen nodded.

"Forgive me if I am wrong, but I suspect that you have something . . . some information . . . some idea of extracting a sum of money from the lady. However, I would guess that you have not worked out your plan in much detail. I say this only because you are young, and my impression is that you have never tried blackmail before."

Hagen tensed. "I didn't say anything about blackmail!"

"No, of course not. You are right to be indignant." Tropard shook his head as if in apology. "Blackmail is an ugly American word. Perhaps I misuse it. My purpose was merely to tell you that if what you want is to see Madame Gilbert, I can arrange such a meeting. We can go to her villa now and be made welcome."

Despite his intention to remain aloof, Hagen could not disguise his surprise.

"She is a former client of mine, and we have remained on

good terms." Tropard straightened his paisley scarf and settled comfortably into the high-backed chair. "Let me explain that I am a businessman. My clients are collectors of objets d'art. They hire me to obtain articles that—for one reason or another—are not for sale. If money were the only consideration, they simply would buy whatever it is they desire. But there are often other problems. Sometimes the objects they covet are owned by someone who does not care to part with them. Sometimes the problems are governmental. Here in Italy, for instance, it is illegal to transport a painting, a document, a sculpture that has reached a certain age—a certain level of antiquity—out of the country. This, you can understand, is inconvenient for my current client, who lives in France and has set his heart upon owning a small Egyptian sculpture that is several hundred years old. At once there is the problem of removing it from Italy, and, added to this, the bronze sculpture is most definitely not for sale."

"I see." Hagen managed a slight conspiratorial grin. "And it belongs to Connie Gilbert."

"Oh, no. Madame Gilbert is a collector of French impressionist paintings. She has never shown any interst in bronzes." Tropard swirled the brandy gently in his glass before taking a sip. "I was able to secure a lovely little Monet for her a few years ago."

"Then the bronze—whatever it is you're after—is owned by Costantino? I thought all the money and the art collection belonged to Mrs. Gilbert."

"And you are correct in half of your assumption."

"I don't understand."

Tropard looked steadily at Hagen before he continued. "At this point," he said, "I think we should come to some sort of agreement. I have been quite open in telling you my intention. Now I need some indication from you that you will consider a joint venture. Are you interested?"

With slight hesitation, Hagen said, "Yes."

"Very well. Long ago I gave up the idea of working totally alone. I no longer have the energy. Besides, the challenge for me is in the planning, not the execution." Tropard smoothed the white hair at his temple. "I recently completed an assignment in Florence for a collector of pen-and-bister drawings of the Italian Renaissance. It was a quite charming work by Ghirlandaio, who, in addition to being a master in his own right, was the teacher of Michelangelo. This fact, however, Ghirlandaio chose to deny, because he was not taken with the study of anatomy, and disapproved of his protégé's fascination with nude bodies." Tropard lit a cigarette and offered one to Hagen, who refused but indulged an older man's digressions. "In any event, none of this has a bearing on our discussion. My point is that I was successful in obtaining that valuable drawing. And the reason for my success was because I enlisted the aid of someone else. You no doubt have noticed the young girl who often accompanies me to St. Mark's Square.

"Yes."

"That is Francesca. She was a novice, like yourself. I sought her out because she had a legitimate backstage job at the Maggio Musciale and was able to discover where the drawing was concealed and how to get to it." Tropard allowed himself a small self-congratulatory laugh. "There was never even a police complaint made by the victim. He could not complain without incriminating himself. He was an American opera singer, and it was well known that he was in Italy for only a brief time. Why would such a man buy an antique work of art that, by law, could not leave the country? Obviously, he intended to take it out illegally. He could hardly explain that to the authorities, could he?" In the manner of an affectionate father, Tropard added, "This should be lesson number one for you, my dear boy. If you are going to steal, steal from a thief. He is not likely to make an issue of it. But about Francesca . . ."

Hagen realized that Tropard was talking as though their partnership were sealed. With a slight inner start of surprise, he admitted to himself that it was.

". . . she, too, will be involved in our joint project. But you and Costantino are the keys. Yes, the two of you are the most important elements, because you both, indirectly, have access to the bronze sculpture."

"I do?" Kyle Hagen could not have been more surprised by anything Tropard might have said.

"The thought of it is almost too much to bear." Tropard clasped his hands together and looked heavenward in near ecstasy. "For a man like me who has spent more than thirty years collecting art—for other people—to gain entry to such a place! It will be the culmination of my life's work."

"What place? What are you talking about?"

"St. Mark's Cathedral, of course. To think of the tapestries, the paintings, the gold, and the jewels! There are pearls by the thousand, hundreds and hundreds of garnets, amethysts, emeralds . . ."

"You're talking about the *Pala d'Oro*. That's crazy." Hagen half-stood to leave. He knew all about the famous Byzantine screen; a sheet of gold and enamel shaped like a cross and studded with precious stones that stood by the high altar in the Basilica of St. Mark's Cathedral. He pointed it out and described it to tour groups every day.

"Wait, my friend. Wait." With a smile, Tropard put his hand on Hagen's shoulder, gently pushing him back into his chair. "The *Pala d'Oro* is not our goal. Nor are any of the fabulous paintings or tapestries. I was merely indulging in a flight of fancy. No, we will not be like Napoleon's soldiers, who gouged out precious stones from the golden screen and dropped them in their pockets. We are after only one thing."

Hagen sat again, watching Tropard.

"Actually, this is another lesson for you," Tropard said. "Never be greedy. My client has requested one object only and has agreed to pay a great deal of money when it is delivered. Believe me, your share will be much more than you would ever have been able to obtain from the penurious Connie Gilbert. She still owes me a final payment for the Monet. No. No matter how tempting it might be to augment our endeavor with other available riches, the only thing we will take is one small, rather ugly, bronze sculpture. Now. How do we go about it? Lesson three: never be in a hurry."

As if to illustrate his last statement, Tropard leisurely served them each three-quarters of an inch of cognac. He held the bowl of his glass in the palms of both hands to warm it before taking a sip. "First," he said, "we must obtain what will undoubtedly be the unwilling cooperation of the director of the Committee for the Preservation of Venetian Art, Monsieur Costantino. Since my instincts tell me that he is content with his life as the protector, lover, and confidant of the wealthy widow Gilbert, a bribe is not practical." For an instant, Tropard's eyes did not shine like those of a kindly mentor, but took on a steeliness sometimes seen at a baccarat table. "We must find a way to bind him to us. This would seem to be where you will be of greatest value."

Tropard fell silent. Hagen was suddenly conscious of the sounds of tinkling glasses being washed behind the bar, low conversation from a group across the way, and the ticking of a cherrywood clock that stood next to the fireplace behind him. It was time for him to speak. He began to describe his meeting in California with Connie Gilbert's daughter, Sandra. He told Tropard about the young woman's suicide and the concern she had expressed to him before her death about her own daughter, who was in the grandmother's custody.

"This child is in school here in Italy?" This question was one of the few times Tropard interrupted Hagen.

"Yes. In Pisa. Sandra had not seen her—Mary Louise is the little girl's name—in over a year."

Hagen spun out his story through another glass of brandy, telling Tropard useless details and concealing, for the time being, a fact that he considered his ace card.

But Tropard was only half-listening after Hagen left the subject of Connie Gilbert's granddaughter. Already the plan he had been searching for was taking shape.

Later, Tropard stood with Hagen in front of the hotel as the tour director waited for the vaporetto.

"It is Costantino who must actually hand the statue to us," Tropard said. Then, putting a friendly hand on Hagen's shoulder he added, "I, too, have some memory of the Book of Mark, my young friend. As I recall, he said, *'No man can enter into a strong man's house, and spoil his goods, except he will first bind the strong man; and then he will spoil his house.'*"

Chapter Seven

As the summer faded, Tropard and Hagen met three more times in the salon of the Mediterraneo Hotel. They invited Francesca Pellegrino to their last meeting, as the role they had invented for her was vital in their plan to steal the Egyptian mask.

Though she was reluctant to go, the first week of October, Francesca was in Pisa, not Paris as Georges Tropard had originally promised.

"Just do this one last thing for me," Tropard had said, "and then we will leave Italy. A week or two from now, at the most."

She did love him, she supposed. She did want to go to Paris, she was sure.

As a child, Francesca had lived in one of the identical small houses provided for employees of the Tuscan winery where her father worked in the vineyards. Until she was twelve, she had gone to the convent school. By then her body had begun to blossom, and her father could tell she would have no trouble getting a husband. Education, therefore, except in her mother's kitchen, was not important.

And for a while she was content to help her mother with the cooking and cleaning, and slip away when she could to play along the edge of the Arno. Francesca had spent many summer days alone on the bank of the river, eating wild grapes and pushing loose pebbles into the water with her bare feet. She had made stick-dolls from the twigs of an olive tree and floated them on grape leaves, sending them with the current, pretending each time that the leaf was a boat carrying her to Florence. She dreamed of working there as a salesgirl in one of the gold and silver shops on the Ponte Vecchio. She could imagine arranging the golden jewelry on a black velvet cushion for the customers to admire; straightening the golden chains with her graceful hands. Her fingernails would be clean and shaped and polished a deep red.

She had realized her dream to be a salesgirl on the Ponte Vecchio, only to discover that what she really wanted was to be on the other side of the counter. She wanted to be one of the women—especially one of the French women in haute couture ensembles—who could afford to buy the gold and silver from the shop where she worked. Perhaps if she were an actress and appeared on the stage in the proper setting under flattering lights—like a golden necklace on black velvet—she would be seen and appreciated.

"You are playing the part of a nun," Tropard had said. "Think of it that way. You're an actress. You told me you didn't want to remain a makeup girl forever."

Alone, in the hotel room in Pisa, as she lifted the nun's habit out of the box from the dry cleaner's shop, the rustle of tissue paper seemed unnaturally loud, almost ominous.

The lingering smell of cleaning fluid on wool filled the room. Well, she had to try the nun's habit on sometime. To be convincing, it must fit properly.

A sudden sound at the window startled her. She turned quickly and saw that it was merely a tree branch brushing against the glass. Here in Pisa, she was acutely aware of small sounds she would not even have heard in Venice. Over the summer she had grown used to the lapping of water against the stone walls of the canals that masked the rustle of branches. The hum of an insect, the ticking of a clock, a distant footstep all seemed to blend with the soft splash of the waterway beneath their hotel window.

But Pisa was too quiet. That was why she was nervous, Francesca told herself. Deliberately, she crumpled the whispering tissue into a ball and tossed it across the room. She listened to it land on the battered dressing table, then fall into the metal trash basket.

With determination she stepped out of her printed dress and high-heeled sandals and stood nude in the center of the room. Barely past her teens, she had nice breasts, but the rest of her body was as slim as a sapling. Her features were pleasant, though unremarkable. What people usually noticed about her was her hair. The abundance of tangled curls suggested that all her body's energy to grow had been concentrated in her scalp. "You're like a tree that needs pruning," Georges Tropard had said.

No. No, it was not Tropard who had said that. It was that American tour director, Kyle Hagen, with whom Tropard had become so friendly.

"Hey, babe, I'm teasing you. Your hair's great." Hagen had laughed and hugged her. And then he had quoted Scripture. He seemed to have a quotation for everything. "You're a living parable of the fig tree. *When her branch is yet tender and putteth forth leaves, ye know that summer is near.* See what I mean?"

"No," she had said, "I don't."

Something else she did not understand was why

Georges Tropard had insisted on including Kyle Hagen in his plan to get the Egyptian bronze mask.

"I can't do it alone," Tropard had told Francesca, "I need your help, and I'll have to hire several other people. One of them may as well be Hagen. Besides, he swears he has a lever to use on Mario Costantino."

"A what?"

"A lever—a key—a last resort, if all else fails. If Costantino will not lead me to the mask down one path, we'll try another."

It had been Hagen's idea that she pose as a nun.

Like diving into a murky pool, she thrust her arms into the sleeves of the black garment. Pulling it over her head, she let the heavy cloth fall loosely around her. The skirt covered the tops of her bare feet, and an extra inch of fabric folded at the floor.

With the white wimple framing her face and the black woolen veil hiding her hair, she turned to study her image in the mirror. She was pleased. No one would question that she was a novice from the Scuola per Bambini.

There was the sound of footsteps in the carpeted hallway.

"Who is it?"

"Kyle."

She undid the latch. "Hurry," she said. "Come in."

With the door locked behind them, Hagen looked at her in surprise and laughed. "You're a picture of purity," he said as she held her arms straight out from her shoulders and turned around in front of him so he could get the full effect. "An absolute Madonna."

"It's a little too long," she said, "but with shoes it will do."

As Hagen watched her practice walking about the room in the nun's habit, he stretched out on the bed, propping a pillow behind his head.

Francesca gave him a quick, stern glance. She did not like the proprietary manner he had developed since they had been in Pisa.

Slightly chastened, he swung his feet to the floor and sat up. "It's perfect," he said. "Now tell me again what you're supposed to do."

"*Cristo*! How many times?"

"At least once more."

This time she had not meant to look in the mirror. She was startled when she glanced in that direction and saw her own face peering back, framed in starched white linen, startled, and a little frightened. Quickly she began to unhook the black veil.

"Where did you get the costume?"

"It's no costume," Francesca said. "It's actually a nun's habit. I stopped in Florence on my way here from Venice. Someone I knew from the Maggio Musicale works in a dry cleaning shop. He'll say it was lost in the main plant."

"Okay, let's hear it," Hagen said, all business now. "Tell me again."

"I wait in the second-class car until the train leaves Florence," Francesca said as she pulled off the wimple and set free her unruly hair. "Then I go to first class . . ."

She continued to describe the plan for kidnapping Connie Gilbert's granddaughter, step by step, in the same monotone in which she had recited catechism when she was twleve years old. "I go to compartment twenty-seven."

"Twenty-seven B."

"Twenty-seven B. I take the rolled-up cotton out of the plastic bag . . ."

"Be sure you wait until you enter the compartment. Don't let anyone else smell it."

"With luck, the old woman will be asleep." Francesca continued by rote. "If she is awake, I hold the cotton over her nose—like this." She reached down and clamped her hand over Kyle Hagen's mouth and nose.

He bit her finger.

"Bastard," she said. "Stop playing games."

"Go on." He patted her thigh through the thick folds of heavy wool.

She moved out of his reach. "Then I do the same to the child." Francesca stopped for a moment, frowning. "You're sure it will only make her sleep?"

"What good would she be to us dead?" Hagen picked up the corner of the bedspread and polished the tops of his shoes. "If you have trouble, there will be others on the train to help you."

"Who?"

"Tropard has hired some guys who have worked for him before. You won't know them, but they will be there."

"Then why can't one of them take her?"

"Don't worry about it," Hagen said. "You'll be fine."

Reluctantly, Francesca nodded. There was no turning back now. She began to tremble a little. She knew that for a crime such as this, there was not only the danger of being caught by the *polizia*. The child at the Scuola per Bambini and her wealthy grandmother were Americans. That made it an international incident.

"Just do everything the way we've rehearsed."

"Yes, of course," she said.

Hagen stood and came toward her. "It seems a shame to waste this hotel room," he said.

"Leave me alone."

"What do you see in an old guy like Tropard?" He laughed and reached for her sleeve, bunching the black wool in his fist. "Still, if you want to, you can pretend I'm your Frenchman, and I'll pretend you're really a nun."

"No." Francesca pushed him away. "You'll get paid for your trouble, but not by me."

Across the Arno River from Francesca's hotel, Connie Gilbert's granddaughter was at choir practice with her class from the Scuola per Bambini.

It was the day before the little girl's seventh birthday. Mary Louise already knew what her best present would be: her grandmother's permission to miss school for the rest of the week. As soon as choir practice was over, she would board a train and ride in a private compartment with a fold-down bed. That was the good part. The bad part was, a nun was going with her. The rest—that she would spend her birthday at her grandmother's villa in Venice—did not matter much one way or the other.

The Scuola per Bambini was a boarding school attended by the daughters of wealthy Italians and the offspring of well-to-do expatriates, foreign businessmen, and diplomats who found it desirable, or necessary, to be in Italy most of the year.

Once each month, the *direttrice di musica* loaded the twenty first-grade girls into the school's Mercedes bus and took them to the Baptistery, one of Pisa's three famous monuments in the Piazza del Duomo, where they would rehearse in the formal setting. Parents and friends were invited to attend this special event, which was meant to be a treat for the children as well as the adults.

The little girls looked forward to the outing because a picnic was included in the day's activities. Checkered cloths were spread, and hampers were opened on the incredibly green expanse of grass that provided the dramatic setting for the three ancient architectural marvels. There were no trees, shrubs, fountains, or statues to distract the eye from the Baptistery, the Cathedral, and the famous leaning Bell Tower.

After lunch, the students who dared were allowed to climb the two-hundred and ninety-four steps to the terrace at the top of the Bell Tower, from which they usually yelled insults to their fainthearted classmates below.

The adults who found time to attend the rehearsal agreed that nowhere else on earth did children's voices sound more beautiful than in the thirteenth-century Baptistery with its unique echo-producing acoustics. The phenomenon was explained scientifically by the placement of the delicate-looking marble columns and the circular design of the sanctuary. The devout, however, said that the sound of an innocent voice raised in song before the magnificent Giovanni Pisano—sculpted pulpit would circle the room at ground level, then spiral upward to the pointed cupola of the ceiling and escape from there to heaven.

This particular Thursday morning, the anthem echoed around the sanctuary and built to a crescendo. As the final phrase faded and floated toward the cupola, one unrehearsed "Gloria!" followed it up.

The music director stared sternly at Connie Gilbert's granddaughter, who had simply wanted to hear the sound of her own voice without the clutter of all the others. Mary Louise, searching the ceiling as though she hoped to catch a glimpse of her voice before it faded away, had to be prompted by her roommate to turn with the others and march from the sanctuary.

As the children approached the doorway of the wood-paneled choir room, the director hurried each child along with a gentle push until Mary Louise was in reach.

"Wait here." The director plucked the little girl from the line and whispered sharply, "Stand next to me until the others are inside."

A second, older nun, making her way slowly from the

outside doorway, asked, "Which one is Signora Gilbert's granddaughter?"

"Over here, Sister Angelica," the choir director answered with a sigh, sorry that a lecture on willful behavior would have to be temporarily postponed.

Sister Angelica's shoulders hunched forward, causing the hem of her black skirt to ride up above the heels of her shoes. "Ah, so this is the bambina," she said, smiling down at the top of the little girl's head. Mary Louise stood no higher than the cross that hung at Sister Angelica's waist.

"I'll be going with you to Venice," Sister Angelica said. "We must hurry and get you packed. Your grandmother would not be happy if we missed the train."

"Yes, Sister," Mary Louise answered, letting herself be hurried from the sanctuary. She looked back over her shoulder at the other girls running toward the picnic site. Too bad she would miss climbing the tower, but at least she had been spared another lecture.

Chapter Eight

It was just before dusk with only pale yellow traces of sunlight remaining on the tallest domes and spires of the city when Andrea Perkins arrived at Stazione Centrale in Florence.

"*Signorina!*" A porter hurried to take her bag as she entered the busy terminal. "*Per favore, signorina!*" He gave Andrea the smile of admiration Italian men bestow on all women, then added the wistful sigh reserved for the real beauties. The sigh, accompanied by a sad shake of the head, implied, "Ah, if only we had met under different circumstances." Or, "If only we were alone!" or "If only I were not already married with three children!"

Since coming to Italy from her native Boston to accept the number two position at the Galleria dell' Accademia, Andrea had become accustomed to the attention her red hair and slim-waisted figure attracted. She had learned to accept the open appraisal from strange men with good humor and also to keep a keen eye on the hands of those who got within pinching distance.

She tipped the porter to load her suitcase onto a luggage cart and dispatch it to—she hoped—the same destination as the passenger car where she had reserved a compartment.

"*E la borza?*" And the hand luggage? The porter reached for the canvas tote bag that Andrea carried.

"No. No, *grazzie.*" Andrea's fingers automatically tightened on the wooden handles. The bag contained her favorite tools among her precious art supplies, and she always carried them herself. Everything in the bag was special to her, the brushes, the palette, the magnifying glass with the tiny battery-powered light, even the rags. They had been seasoned by long hours spent lovingly restoring treasured old works of art and skeptically examining others whose value was questionable. To Andrea, her equipment was like antique silver that takes on a special patina and becomes more valuable with use.

The *rapido* train had just majestically entered the station and was demanding attention. It was a sleek Italian adjunct of the Trans-Europe Express. The *rapido* began its run where the French train that served the Golfe du Lion and the Côte d'Azur left off. At the end of the Italian spur's line was Venice, Andrea's destination.

For personal as well as professional reasons, Andrea looked forward to her project with the Committee for the Preservation of Venetian Art. Venice was her favorite of all cities, and her favorite of all men—Aldo Balzani—would be there with her, however briefly. He had admitted, to her coaxing, that the Florentine Police Department could function without its captain of detectives for at least two days.

Balzani was not exactly late; there was still plenty of time, Andrea told herself. It was foolish to start worrying that something had come up at the last minute to prevent their being together in Venice. Nevertheless, she chose a seat in the waiting room where she had a view of the clock and of the parking lot where he would arrive.

Unlike most things in Italy, the trains ran on schedule. One could depend on arriving and departing at the times listed in the timetable. And though, at the moment, Andrea's only concern was when they would leave Florence, the *rapido*'s entire route that particular day in October became important to both Andrea and Balzani. The stops the train made to take on passengers and to load cargo involved them both, later, in a pitiful little murder.

The *rapido*'s schedule was designed for passengers in a hurry, not sightseers, even though its route was along the Italian Riviera and through an extraordinary stretch of scenery. The starting point was near Nice at the French and Italian border. Once out of the station, the train whizzed past San Remo's resort hotels, lavish yacht facilities, and glorious beaches without stopping until it reached Genoa. The only other stop before reaching Florence was at Pisa. Among those who came on board there were a little girl and a nun from the nearby Scuola per Bambini.

At Florence, the train took on cargo as well as passengers.

For a while, Andrea watched without interest as the freight cars were being loaded. Then she checked the clock again and the parking lot, as though merely watching for Aldo Balzani's car would make it arrive more quickly.

Suddenly the sound of screeching brakes and grinding metal diverted her attention back to the loading zone.

A large delivery van had pulled left too quickly and scraped against a flatbed truck. The van was packed to the roof with stringbeans in straw baskets blocking the windows. The driver apparently had not seen the other vehicle approaching in the lane beside him until it was too late.

Not only did the collision dent the cab of the oncoming

truck and scrape off half the letters of *The Brufanti Olive Company* painted on its side, but the impact sent a number of empty barrels careening around the side-rails of the open flatbed and banging into the three men who were riding in the back. The men, all dressed in the green coveralls of warehouse workers, instantly jumped over the tailgate to the ground with a great deal of shouting and fist waving.

The guilty driver of the other vehicle reluctantly stopped his van and climbed down. Holding his hands out in front of him and hunching his shoulders, he looked skyward as though questioning why some outside force had rammed his vehicle into the other one. With very little confidence in this ploy as a defense, however, he stayed close to the open door of the van in case his only recourse was a hurried getaway.

Then an astonishing thing happened. Someone from inside the dented cab of the truck shouted, *"Calmi! Ritornare!"*

Almost at once, the men who had been riding in the flatbed jumped back on. Then the driver shifted into gear and sped away.

Andrea was as surprised as the driver of the van, who clearly had been at fault, that the incident had ended so quickly and with so few recriminations.

Later, with the clear recall of an uninvolved bystander, Andrea found that the scene was locked in her memory. The perplexed driver of the van, the dented truck, the green coveralls, the careening olive barrels were all there. But for the moment, she quickly forgot the accident when she felt a familiar kiss on the back of her neck.

"Are you the lady who was looking for a policeman?" Aldo Balzani turned her by the shoulders and kissed her mouth.

"I was beginning to think it was true that you can never find one when you want him."

"It depends a lot on what you want him for." Balzani said, smiling. He put his arm around her waist and they started toward the train.

Aldo Balzani's English had the soft sibilants of an American southern accent, which he had acquired during his school years in New Orleans where he had lived with his grandmother. His Italian was native and rich with the Florentine colloquialisms he had learned in his father's home as a small child.

"You don't have a suitcase," Andrea said.

"I was afraid you'd notice that."

"How could I not notice?" Andrea had a sinking feeling. Something had come up.

"No one else has mentioned it."

He tried to hurry her toward the train. She tried to slow the pace.

"You have a keen sense of observation," he said.

"Something's happened, hasn't it?"

"It's the artist's eye, I suppose," he said, evading the question. "I've always admired your ability to sum up a situation at a glance. An attractive quality. Not as attractive as your red hair and green eyes but definitely more appealing than your singing voice."

"Aldo. You're not coming with me, are you?"

He stopped and took hold of both her hands. "No."

"We're going to miss Venice again." Andrea had lost track of the number of times she and Balzani had planned a trip to Venice, which one or the other of them had always had to cancel at the last minute. She felt like crying. She felt like smashing his nose, and *then* crying.

"I may be able to join you tomorrow," he started to explain but was overpowered by an announcement over the loudspeaker that the train was ready for boarding. Balzani started again. "There's a report that the makeup girl from the Maggio Musicale was seen in Florence a day or so ago. I've got to check it out."

"Can't someone else do it?" They were standing near the door of the first-class car. Passengers eager to board moved around them as though Andrea and Balzani were rocks diverting a stream.

"It's my case. It could be just another false lead." Then, in a casual tone meant to convince Andrea—and himself—he said, "There's a good chance I can be in Venice by tomorrow evening."

The conductor motioned impatiently for the few remaining stragglers to get on board.

Balzani put his hands on Andrea's shoulders and bent down so that their faces were level. "I'm sorry, darlin'."

Andrea knew that was true. She would have felt better if she could have yelled, Why does it always have to be you? But she had learned not to ask questions like that. They only gave him permission to question her the same way. Why had she gone to Ferrara to restore a sixteenth-century fresco when he had three free days? Why had she stayed in Florence to examine a fake portrait by Botticelli when they had made plans to hear *Rigoletto* in Milan?

"Tomorrow?" She felt like a fool when she heard the pleading tone in her voice.

"I'll be there if there is any way at all." He touched her cheek, then smoothed a stray strand of coppery hair behind her ear.

"Signore, signorina!" the conductor shouted. "*Presto, presto!*"

Balzani kissed Andrea soundly, lifted her onto the high metal step of the coach, then hurried back through the crowded terminal.

Andrea stood on the step, looking after him, until she

felt the conductor tug at her sleeve. "Twenty-seven A," he said, "third door down the corridor."

By the time she had taken off her coat and settled in her seat, the sun was gone and the window was silvered with the gray light of evening. She saw her unhappy face reflected there. Suddenly, beyond her shoulder, she saw another face, a small and round one with large blue eyes framed by tousled yellow curls. Andrea turned and smiled at the little girl.

"You're an American, aren't you?" Connie Gilbert's granddaughter, Mary Louise, came into the compartment and climbed up on the opposite seat.

"How can you tell?"

"I can *read*," Mary Louise said indignantly, as though she had been mistaken for someone many years her junior. She touched Andrea's Bloomingdale's tote bag with her foot and said, "My grandmother ordered these shoes from there." Then she held her legs straight out, showing off white patent-leather pumps with white grosgrain ribbons.

"Do you live in New York?"

"I don't know *where* I live." The child gave a shrug of great boredom and rolled her eyes in an exaggerated fashion. "I live wherever they put me. I've been going to a stupid school in Pisa, but now, when I see my grandmother, I think I'm going to live in Venice."

The train lurched, then moved slowly forward. As they passed through the freight area, Andrea saw that the dented truck was still there. As she watched, a young man in green coveralls jumped into the cab and drove toward the main exit onto the Via Nazionale. The other men who had ridden in back were gone. As far as Andrea could tell, no new cargo had been loaded on the flatbed. She wondered how the driver was going to explain the smashed-in cab to his boss at the Brufanti Olive Company.

The little girl across from Andrea picked at a loose

thread on the arm of the seat. "I saw you out the window before you got on the train. Was that your boyfriend you were kissing?"

"Yes," Andrea answered, turning her attention back to her young companion.

"None of the nuns at school have boyfriends. They're not allowed. At least that's what a twelve-year-old girl on the second floor said."

Andrea smiled.

"She says they're all celibate, whatever that means." She looked at Andrea as though she expected her to supply the definition.

"Maybe your mother will explain it for you."

"It's not likely," she said with a sigh of bored resignation that lifted her shoulders. "She's in California. *I* don't even remember what she looks like." Turning her attention again to the upholstered armrest, she began poking at the tiny hole that the pulled thread had created, enlarging the tear with her index finger.

"Is your father on the train with you?" Andrea could not imagine that an American child this young was traveling alone.

"Not likely," she said, obviously fond of the phrase. "I don't even *know* where he is."

"You're not here by yourself, are you?"

"No. Some nun from the school brought me," she said, intent on pulling out little wisps of cotton stuffing and dropping them on the floor. "She went to the ladies."

"Oh, I see."

"They all speak Italian."

"Yes, I imagine. Do you?"

"When I want to. Some of them could speak English if they *tried*, but they won't." Then, with hardly a pause to indicate there was a change of topic, "Do you know what the

Mother Superior told me . . . *in* Italian?" She looked directly at Andrea as though the Reverend Mother might have taken this stranger into her confidence.

"No, I don't." Andrea grinned. She liked the little girl and her directness.

"She told me my mother was with the *angels*," the girl said, rolling her eyes. "But I'll tell you what *I* think. I think she's dead."

Andrea instinctively reached out to lift the child onto the seat beside her. How long had it been, she wondered, since someone had merely held the little girl and stroked her hair.

"*Bambina!*" A nun stood in the shadows outside the doorway. Sister Angelica always sought the shadows. "You must sleep," she said to the child in Italian. "Otherwise you will be cranky when we meet your grandmother."

In the thirty years since Sister Angelica had taken the veil, she had never had a single doubt about the way she had chosen to spend her life. She had served with obedience and with a modesty that was admired by all those who served with her.

Her humility had developed from an early acquaintance with pain and mortification. At the age of ten, in a kitchen accident, boiling water had spilled across her chest. Even when the physical pain was gone, and fragile new skin had grown back and covered her rib cage, the mental anguish remained. Though only her mother knew how extensive the scarring was, by the time the girl reached puberty, she habitually hunched her shoulders forward and wore high-necked blouses even on the hottest days of summer. And when she decided to become a nun and serve God, she was grateful His uniform drew so little attention to the woman who wore it.

In the last few years she had found almost perfect peace. Now that her mother was no longer living, only Sister

Angelica herself and God knew of the disfiguring scars on her chest.

The train whistled and gained speed as they left the suburbs of the city.

"*Bambina. Presto!*" Sister Angelica clapped her hands and Mary Louise reluctantly stood to leave.

When she was gone, Andrea dozed in the rhythmic monotony of the sound and movement of the train. She woke once when they stopped briefly in Bologna and once when the whistle blew a warning as the *rapido* approached a small town. Later, she was vaguely aware that the door of the compartment next to hers opened and closed. But then she slept again until she heard the conductor knock at her door and announce, "Venezia—Stazione Centrale."

Quickly brushing her hair, Andrea glanced in the reflection of the window and decided not to bother with lipstick.

The door to 27 B was still closed when she went by. Andrea thought of looking in on the little girl but decided against it. The nun had not encouraged friendship.

The station was busy and noisy. Andrea made her way through the crowd toward the baggage area. As she rummaged in her shoulder-strap purse for the claim ticket, the tote bag slipped from her hand and clattered at her feet. Two paint brushes and her magnifying glass spilled out. She had stopped to retrieve them and had started to rise when she felt a coarse fabric brush agains ther cheek as someone moved past. Standing, she saw the back of a nun's habit in front of her and the little girl from the train, eyes closed, with her head resting on the woman's shoulder.

"Hello, there!" Andrea reached forward to touch the tangled curls of her earlier visitor, but she was too late: the shoulder where the child's head rested was already out of reach.

With her Bloomingdale's tote bag now firmly in hand,

Andrea smiled in disbelief as she watched the child being carried so rapidly though the crowd. Though Andrea had not actually seen the face of the nun as she stood in the shadowed corridor of the train, there was something about the timbre of the voice and hunch of the shoulders that suggested an elderly woman. But *this* woman was straight and swift as she maneuvered through the crowd, carrying the deadweight of the sleeping child toward the revolving door at the back of the station.

Chapter Nine

Shifting Connie Gilbert's granddaughter to her other shoulder, Francesca Pellegrino hurried along the outside platform behind the Stazione di Santa Lucia to a terrace that was washed by the dark water of the Grand Canal. The lights that lined the dock were yellow and diffused in the nighttime mist and cast sinister-looking shadows on the faces of the passersby.

Even with shoes, the nun's habit still felt too long and Francesca was afraid she might step on the hem and stumble.

Where was Tropard? Francesca felt a surge of panic. Tropard was supposed to be here. He was supposed to meet her as soon as she came out of the station.

Passengers who already had collected their luggage were crowding together in the roped-off area of the platform in front of the *vaporetto*, the water-bus, that would take them to their hotels. The ticket-seller, when he saw Francesca standing uncertainly at the edge of the crowd, removed his hat and said, *"Buona sera, suora."*

Francesca felt weak. Her temples started to pound when she realized that the man was speaking to her. He thought she was a nun; he had addressed her as *Sister*. Further, he seemed determined to use her presence as an opportunity to show his authority to the impatient tourists. He motioned them to stand back and insisted that Francesca and the sleeping child should be first on board.

"No. No, *grazie*." She began to tremble but managed a nervous smile and fled to a bench outside the boarding area.

When all the seats were filled on the *vaporetto* and it glided out into the canal, Francesca saw an Evinrude cruiser that had been blocked from her view before by the larger boat. As the six-passenger outboard came nearer the dock she could see that it was empty except for the driver, whom she recognized. It was Kyle Hagen. But where was Tropard?

Suddenly, from behind, she felt a hand clamp down on her shoulder. Her gasp of surprise was almost a scream.

"Be quiet! It's me." Tropard slid onto the bench beside her. His white hair was covered by a black watch cap and he wore dark pants and a dark sweater.

"Where have you been? You were supposed to meet me outside the door!"

"I had business."

"Business! What business? Someone could have recognized the child—or me!"

"Calm down. I knew you were all right. I watched until you were safely out of the station, then I had to go help unload the cargo."

"What do you mean?"

"Stop talking." Tropard left the bench and ran to the dock to grab the rope Hagen threw to him. As he secured it to the piling he turned back to Francesca. "Come on. Get in." He climbed over the side of the sleek craft that had *Villa Constance* written in gold script on the side, then reached up to take the child.

"No!" Francesca held fast to the little girl.

"Let me have her!"

"I can manage."

"All right, just get in!" Tropard roughly grabbed Francesca's arm to steady her as she stepped down.

Swaying with the rocking boat, she laid the unconscious child on the long narrow seat in the back.

"When you were leaving the station," Tropard said, "who was that woman who tried to speak to you?"

Francesca smoothed the skirt of the nun's habit under her then lifted the little girl's head and cradled it in her lap. She held one hand on the child's chest for a moment. "I can hardly feel her breathing."

"Who was she?" Tropard reached back and grabbed Francesca's wrist. "The woman with the red hair?"

"I don't know what you're talking about," she said, trying to shake free.

"As you came through the waiting room, a woman tried to speak to you—as though she knew who you were."

"I didn't see anyone. Let's go. No one could see my face."

Tropard released his grip. He leaned forward and spoke softly to Hagen, then jumped back onto the dock.

"Where are you going?" Francesca swung around, reaching for the back of his sweater, but was a moment too late. He already was unwrapping the rope from the piling.

"You'll be fine. Hagen knows where to take you. You can manage by yourself until tomorrow."

As the boat pulled away, Francesca's protests were stirred in the sound of the muttering motor and the lapping water.

Tropard began to retrace his steps. He did not hurry. Staying on the outside of the walkway, he carefully avoided the crowd, and entered the baggage area once again. No one took notice of him. Certainly Andrea Perkins was not aware that he stopped behind a loaded luggage cart and listened as she gave a porter her name and instructions on where to send her suitcase.

Her name sounded familiar, Tropard thought as he made for the exit that led to the freight yard. And he was sure he had seen her somewhere before. It would come to him when he had time to think about it. At the moment he had a more immediate problem to solve.

Outside, from beneath the second freight car of the *rapido*, he pulled a paper sack he had hidden earlier. The sack was heavier than it looked, and he held it waist high, using both hands.

Slowly, crossing the darkened tracks and taking care not to stumble on the rails, he reached the bridge that linked the train yard with the maritime station.

Tropard checked to make sure there was no one nearby, then sat on the bank and removed the contents from the bag: some bulky clothing that smelled of harsh soap and arthritis ointment, a rosary, and a tire jack.

Folding the smaller garments and the rosary inside the black woolen dress, he wrapped them around the jack and tied them with a length of nylon rope he took from his pocket. Placing them once again inside the bag, Tropard walked to the center of the bridge and dropped the bundle over the edge.

No matter how often Andrea came to Venice, she would never get used to stepping out of an ordinary Italian train station and, instead of hailing a taxi, stepping into a waiting gondola.

There it was, all around her. The Venice of books and art galleries; the old palaces in faded pearl shades of green and brown and Venetian red, the stripped mooring poles, and black gondolas. For Andrea, the city was more magical in the misty October evening than in the silken shine of sunlight that had delighted Venetian artists for centuries.

I'm warning you, Aldo Balzani, she thought as she settled into the black leather seat and listened to the miniature waves of the shallow water splash against the dark hull of the boat. *All this romance is too good to waste. If you don't show up, I'm going to make a fool of myself over the first handsome Venetian that comes close enough.*

Andrea kicked off her shoes and dug her toes into the soft carpet. Ahead, she could see the hazy outline of the dome of Saint Mark's and the Bell Tower. Gondolas in the Grand Canal crossed and recrossed their own wavering reflections. *Vaporetti* sped by, then slowed and stopped along the way at glassed-in waiting rooms on floating landing stages.

When they reached the Piazza San Marco, the gondolier guided his craft between two mooring poles. He leaped to the dock and extended a hand to help her. "Signorina, your hotel is through the square, the first street on the left."

"Yes, I know," she said, and expressed her thanks with a more than generous tip.

Music from a nearby veranda floated with the mist across the canal. First an accordian played a solo introduction, then a guitar added background and a mandolin began the melody of "Musetta's Waltz."

And if he can play a mandolin, she thought as she started across the square, *you're in real trouble, Balzani.*

Georges Tropard went up the service stairs to his room at the Mediterraneo. He took off his watch cap and dark clothes, and by the time he had finished his shower, he calculated that Kyle Hagen should have returned to his own hotel. Tropard dialed and asked for Hagen's room.

"Hagen."

"Did it go as we planned?" Tropard rubbed his white hair with a towel.

"Exactly."

"Francesca and the little girl?"

"They're safely inside the villa."

"And the boatman?"

"I paid him for the use of the boat, and told him he'd get the rest of his money after we used it again."

"What about Mrs. Gilbert?"

Hagen hesitated. "I can't say how she'll be tomorrow, but at least everything's all right so far."

Tropard was confident that Francesca could handle the grandmother. "There *were* two unexpected problems . . ."

"What? What problems?" Hagen's nervousness was evident in his voice.

Tropard answered him sternly. "You may have to deal with this first one alone, so listen carefully." After a pause, Tropard continued. "There was a woman on the train. An American. She may have seen something or talked to them." Tropard described seeing Andrea reach out toward Francesca and say something to her as she carried the unconscious child through the train station. "Her name is Andrea Perkins, and she's registered at your hotel."

"What do you want me to do?"

"Nothing yet." After another pause, Tropard said evenly, "There can't be any witnesses."

Hagen did not answer.

"There's more than money at stake now," Tropard said.

"What do you mean?"

"I'll explain it to you in the morning."

"I'd rather know now," Hagen said, but the phone was already dead.

Chapter Ten

The olive barrel that was dropped into the Canale di Fusina that night by two men in green coveralls should have sunk beneath the cloudy water and stayed undetected until the canal was dredged or until the tide carried it past the Lido and into the Adriatic. That was what was meant to happen. As a precaution, after the barrel was sealed, holes were bored in the side and an opening was knocked in the lid with a hammer. The theory was that water would rush in and cover the contents, thus forcing out the air, and the cask would drop to the bottom like a stone.

A safe distance from shore, the barrel was eased over the side by the two men in the boat. They were careful not to cause a loud splash that would attract attention. Rolling and dipping, it drifted away from the idling boat. Though the night was too dark to see bubbles rising, there was a gurgling sound as water rushed in to fill the cavities.

Both men were understandably nervous and anxious to get away, and once the barrel was no longer visible, the driver threw the control into high gear and they fled toward the Grand Canal. What they did not realize was that the turbulence caused by the outboard motor buffeted the barrel in the wake, displacing enough of the water so that the wooden container began to float and bob like a buoy.

The cask might still have reached the open sea by floating with the tide had it not been spotted, a few hours later, in the bright light of a patrol boat from the Bacino Della Stazione Marittima.

The small crew thought they recognized the object immediately. With speed and skill, and not a little enthusiasm, they maneuvered their small craft next to what they assumed was the serendipitous discovery of a wayward barrel of wine which had fallen, no doubt, from a passing delivery boat.

Using a net and a sturdy harpoonlike hook, the seamen hauled the barrel to the edge of their open boat. It took two of them to lift it. But to the sailors' disappointment, once the cask was out of the water they discovered the hole in the top and watched wordlessly as water poured back into the canal.

Tilting the barrel until it was drained, they deposited it on its side in the bottom of the boat. It was heavy—too heavy to be empty—and out of having nothing more interesting to do, one man reached for a chisel and a hammer to remove the lid, the other trained a flashlight on the top.

Something—it appeared to be a nylon rope—was dangling from the hole in the lid. The man with the flashlight absently pulled at it with his free hand. Then, suddenly he dropped the light and let it clatter to the bottom of the boat. The maritime patrolman's whole body jerked backward in repulsion when he realized what he had touched. It was a twisted gray mass made lank and slippery by the cold water of the canal. It felt almost weightless in his open hand as the tendrils spread and dripped between his fingers, and he knew at once that what he held was a hank of human hair.

In Florence, Chief of Detectives Aldo Balzani had spent the first part of that same evening trying to follow up on the lead that the makeup girl from the Maggio Musicale had been seen in Florence.

The desk sergeant had taken the call from someone named Stefano (no last name or telephone number) who worked at the Bavio Cleaners. By the time Balzani got the message the dry cleaner's shop was closed for the day and no one was answering the phone. When he drove to the address, only the night watchman was there and he did not have a list of the employees.

From there, he went to stake out the Ponte Vecchio, the covered bridge across the Arno that for centuries has been the location of shops occupied by Florentine goldsmiths and jewelry merchants, and of late, the target of a well-organized band of thieves. Balzani stationed one man on each side of the river while he sat in the darkened back room of one of the shops.

The only disturbances all night were the crashing of a beer bottle thrown from a passing car against the stone walkway, and the desperate squeak of a rat caught in the wire screen beneath the bridge.

Balzani stood and stretched. A first ray of sunlight angled in through the small window at the back of the shop and was caught and scattered among the gold necklaces in the jewler's display case.

Balzani locked the shop and sent his men home. As he started the short walk to his own apartment, he poked his wrinkled shirt into his pants and halfheartedly straightened the jacket of his brown suit. His brown suit was almost exactly like his tan suit and his navy blue suit. All of them were durable worsted, all came from the rack marked *Tall Sizes*, and they all fit without alterations. His shirts were white, his ties were subdued, and all his socks were black or brown. Balzani was not a sartorial dazzler, nor did he care to be. On mornings like this he was tempted to substitute tennis shoes for his heavy wing-tips.

He was tired. The night had been wasted. The stake-out was pointless. At the corner as he waited for the light to change he looked back at the Ponte Vecchio, at the small shops precariously cantilevered from the bridge to jut out above the Arno that rushed beneath. The just-emerging sun tinted the scene in shades of pink with yellow highlights as bright as Florentine gold-leaf. This early in the morning, before the shopkeepers and tourists were out, one would not have been surprised to see Cosimo de Medici emerge from the half-mile corridor that had spanned the river since the sixteenth century. The Medici clan would still feel at home in Florence, Balzani thought. But what the hell was *he* doing here?

Balzani crossed the street, almost colliding with a Vespa motor scooter that wheeled around the corner against the light. Bereft of his mother in his early childhood, the young Aldo had been sent to live in America. He had grown up in New Orleans in the home of his grandmother, whose concern for him had been, for the most part, that he always had enough pasta and spinach. His first visit as an adult to his father's family in Italy had overwhelmed him. The hugging, kissing, singing, and laughing of the near and distant relatives had opened the blocked-off spaces inside him. He was delighted with the ever-present children and with their mothers who did not plan the number of offspring but nurtured them all as gifts from God. His uncles, who provided for the large households, accepted as their due the uncontested role of *capo*, leader, and *giudice*, judge. Or so it all seemed to the young American cousin at those first family gatherings.

Balzani had come to Italy to celebrate a master's degree in political science from Tulane University, which had been much harder to get than his football conference-championship ring that had impressed his father more. It was supposed to have been only a vacation. That was five years ago. So, he asked himself, why the hell was he still in Italy?

To begin with, at his family's urging, he had taken a job inherited from his father on the Florentine police force. Then, instead of finding a nice Italian girl whose view of the future was the same as one of his aunts—which was vaguely what Balzani had in mind—he had met Andrea Perkins. He had fallen in love with an American girl who had one more college degree than he did, who was not yet ready to get married, and who was not in a hurry to have children even when she did. He could have stayed in New Orleans and done that.

Balzani took the three flights of stairs to his apartment instead of waiting for the elevator that probably was not working anyway. By the time he reached the last landing he was breathing hard and holding on to the banister. When Andrea was with him they ran all the way up. She had stamina. More than he did sometimes. He unlocked his door and went into his *appartamento efficiente*, as his landlord optimistically called the cramped two rooms and bath. And Andrea had heart, as his football coach used to say when he meant guts. She had guts, all right. She had almost gotten herself killed more than once since she had been working at the Accademia.

Balzani stripped off his clothes, hanging his brown suit on a wooden hanger, and dropping his shirt and underwear in the hamper in the bathroom. The hot water and the steam in the shower began to loosen the knots in his shoulders. He reached for the soap. It was Andrea's; it smelled like peaches. It smelled like her. He closed his eyes and let the water splash full in his face. Rubbing the bar of soap across his chest, he wished they were her hands, not his. He thought of her standing behind him, her lips pressed between his shoulder blades, her arms reaching around lathering his chest . . .

Oh, hell, he said out loud, finishing with the soap and rinsing off in record time. As he grabbed a towel and wrapped it around him the phone rang. Leaving wet footprints on the thin carpet he went to answer.

"Balzani," he said impatiently.

"Aldo, my friend. This is—"

Balzani knew who it was: Georgio Conti from the Venetian Police Department. "Yeah, Georgio."

"It has been too long since we've seen you. When are you coming to Venice?"

"I was just thinking about that very thing."

The amenities out of the way, Conti continued. "I left this information with your office, but I always like to talk with the *capo.*"

"What's up?"

"Two men from the maritime station made a most interesting find while they were on patrol last night. They spotted what they thought was a wine barrel floating in the Canale di Fusina. But when they got it on their boat and opened it, instead of the Chianti they had hoped to find, there was the body of a woman. Her throat had been cut."

"Have you identified her?" Balzani sat quickly on the edge of the bed. How many women were there in Venice at any given time? Why was he immediately frightened for Andrea?

"No. Only that she appears to be between fifty and sixty years old."

Balzani relaxed. "You've already reported this to our Missing Persons?"

"Yes."

"They'll check it out for you."

"I know, Aldo, but it may be your business, too. She may have been murdered in Florence."

"Why? Do you have clothing labels or . . ."

"No clothing at all. Whoever did this wanted to make our job as difficult as possible. The only lead we have is the barrel itself. It's from the Brufanti Olive Company—in Florence."

"I see. I'll check with the Brufanti people."

"The woman should be easy enough to identify."

"How's that?"

"She has no . . . no bosoms. Nothing. Her chest is just scars. Old scars that have been there a long time." A fog horn blared in the background and the Venetian police officer waited until it stopped before he continued. "Anyone who knew the woman well enough to report her missing—a husband, family members—would know about that."

But the only one who had ever seen Sister Angelica without clothes was God.

Chapter Eleven

That same morning, Andrea awoke early. Though her appointment with Mario Costantino—the chairman of the Committee for the Preservation of Venetian Art—was not until nine, she was dressed and eager to leave the Hamilton Plaza Hotel an hour before.

She disliked staying in American hotels in Italy. They were too impersonal, too sanitary, too new. But the Committee had made the reservation at the Hamilton because of its convenient location adjacent to a storage building used by the diocese of Saint Mark's. The building, Mario Costantino had told her, contained a well-lighted workroom with a porcelain sink and two-twenty electrical outlets with built-in adapters. Ideal, he had said, for her investigation.

The Hamilton Plaza was a renovated seventeenth-century palace. The present owners, following a city ordinance, had left the façade intact so that, from the front courtyard, the hotel—with its Byzantine arched windows and marble columns supported by carved winged-lions—harmonized with the architecture in the rest of the city. However, when the hotel chain had bought the crumbling structure, the dilapidated interior had been immediately gutted and the three floors had been fitted with almost identical rooms. Each had a private bath, air-conditioning, a double bed, a Modigliani print on the wall, Monsanto carpet on the floor, and color TV with a list of American movies available on videotape.

In the lobby, Andrea stepped around a group wearing badges that identified them as members of an airline package tour. They were lining up for their promised continental breakfast. A blond tour director in a blue uniform that had been altered to show off her small waist and full breasts stood in the dining-room doorway with a clipboard, checking off names and dispensing "Good mornings" to her charges. Next to her stood a tall, slightly rumpled young man with a closed red, white, and blue umbrella who added his own greetings as well as whispered comments to the blonde as each guest passed by.

He had been watching for Andrea. He had checked her room number at the desk and had a description from Tropard. When Hagen saw Andrea cross the lobby, he interrupted his halfhearted flirtation and casually followed her outside and around the corner to St. Mark's Square. Staying well back, he watched as she was seated at one of the small tables near the bandstand facing the Basilica and was served coffee and a sticky roll by a white-jacketed waiter from the Quadri restaurant.

This early, only a few other customers were seated at the scores of tiny outdoor tables. Andrea watched as the vendors and street photographers began to ready their staked-out territory for the busy day that, so far, promised fragile autumn sunshine. At her feet a dozen pigeons nodded and pressed forward waiting for the crumbs from her roll that they were confident she would throw to them.

The marble paving-stones of the square were still wet from overnight rain and reflected the images of the bell tower and cathedral at one end, and the lacy archways of the buildings on the other three sides. The effect made Andrea feel she was caught at the fold line of a strangely repeated horizon.

She wanted to claim as her own the response of everyone she saw around her. She wanted to be the gray-haired lady seated with her husband a few tables away and to know, after so many years of living together, what he was feeling merely by the pressure of his hand on her shoulder. She wanted to be the young mother in the middle of the square, holding to the waistband of her small son to give him courage as he scattered corn for the greedy gray birds. She wanted to experience the fervor she saw in the wrinkled face of an old priest who crossed himself and gazed at the winged lion of Saint Mark on the clock tower, and to feel the inspiration of the scruffy artist who gazed from his canvas at the stately bronze horses on the Basilica's west façade. But most of all, she wanted to be the girl in the shadow of one of the pillars who held her lover's arm with both hands and turned impulsively to hide her face in his chest as though the scene was just too much to take in all at one time.

Damn you, Aldo Balzani, Andrea thought. Why aren't you here? Why isn't being in Venice with me more important than anything else you have to do? She put her cup down with more force than she intended, spilling coffee and rattling the saucer.

Without her being aware, Kyle Hagen had come from beneath the archway and was standing beside her table. When he spoke, Andrea looked up sharply in surprise, shading her eyes with her hand, though the sun was not that bright.

"You look like someone who's trying to put new wine into old bottles," Kyle Hagen said.

"I beg your pardon?" Andrea frowned, not pleased at having a stranger intrude upon her morning.

Pulling out the chair across from hers but remaining standing, he said in an oratorical manner, ". . . and then Saint Mark said, *'And no man putteth new wine into old bottles: else the new wine doth burst the bottles, and the wine is spilled.'* "

Andrea's first thought was that in a moment he would hand her a pamphlet and ask for a donation. But there was no glint of fanaticism in his eyes, rather, he seemed to be enjoying some private joke at her expense.

He was obviously an American, but without the paraphernalia of a tourist—no guide book, no knapsack, no camera. He was wearing corduroy trousers and a turtleneck sweater—both of which had obviously seen several seasons—but gave the impression of being worn for comfort, not because they represented his entire wardrobe. Looking at him more closely, Andrea decided he was younger than she had thought at first, perhaps even younger than she. But it was the confident way he watched Andrea's reaction that led her to ask, "Is that a new opening routine you're trying out or does it mean something?"

"It means two things, actually." Hagen signaled the waiter to bring another cup and a pot of coffee, then seated himself at Andrea's table. "It means you shouldn't try to pour the present into the past, which, unless I'm mistaken, is what you were doing. And, of lesser importance," Hagen thanked the waiter and refilled Andrea's cup and then his own before continuing, "it means that I can come up with a quotation from the Book of Mark for any occasion."

"Even if it doesn't fit." Andrea was not willing to admit

that he had come close to reading her mood. "Are you a minister?"

"No, I'm a tour director." He held up a plastic-encased card that bore the emblem of a tourist guide organization and a scrawled signature beneath printed lines of identification. He made it a comic gesture like a B-movie detective flashing his badge. "But, yes," he said seriously, returning the card to his pocket, "I am ordained."

Andrea laughed. "You're an ordained tour director?"

"I was a minister before I was a tour director. The ordination came first," he said lightly. "It came in the mail, to be exact. A certificate in a nine-by-twelve envelope. When I was ten years old."

"Something you ordered from a cereal box?"

"No, it was real," he said seriously. Then, "Where are you from?"

"Mostly Boston."

"You came here directly from Boston?"

"No. From Florence."

"On the train?"

"Yes, on the train."

"Did you have a nice trip?"

"It was fine."

"And you're staying at the Hamilton Plaza. I saw you in the lobby. Are you on vacation? I could give you a tour." He flashed his I.D. card again.

"No, I'm here on business, and I have an appointment . . ." The conversation seemed to be taking the turn of an ordinary pick-up. Andrea reached for her purse.

Hagen pretended not to notice her intention to leave and poured more coffee into her almost full cup. "If you're mostly from Boston," he said, talking quickly, "then it's possible that you never heard of mail-order preachers. Maybe they only operate in the midwestern states. That's how I got my certificate. It was my father's idea to get me ordained. He's a minister and had three deacons of his church write letters of recommendation for me. Actually, he didn't have to go to all that trouble." Hagen picked up his umbrella, which he had dropped at his feet and hung it on the back of his chair. "About the recommendations, I mean. I knew of a woman named Hattie Moffit who sent in nothing but the name of her nearest and dearest, Andrew Moffit—and the usual fee, of course—and within a week a certificate came back entitling Andrew to preach the Gospel and call himself pastor. As far as I know, Andrew Moffit is the only fox terrier in Gothan, Missouri, that has the title Reverend preceding his name on his dog tag."

Andrea laughed and shook her head at being taken in.

"It's the truth," Hagen insisted.

"Was the content of your sermons about on a par with the Reverend Andrew Moffit's?"

"No, what I had to say was the Gospel, all right." With surprising hopefulness, he said, "I don't suppose you ever saw me on television."

"Not that I remember." Andrea thought of leaving again, but it was too early to meet Costantino.

"No, of course not. You wouldn't have seen me unless you lived in southwest Missouri. It was just a local station. I didn't actually preach, I just recited Scripture. But one of the networks did a fifteen-minute news documentary on me once. I thought you might have seen that."

"I'm sorry I missed it." Andrea tore off small pieces of her uneaten roll and scattered them for the pigeons.

"I was a freaky kid with a weird memory. For the good of my eternal soul, my dad used to make me memorize Bible verses. Naturally, I thought the faster I learned them, the faster I could get away from the old sonofabitch. I got so I could hear them one time through and quote them back. But that wasn't good enough. My righteous father thought, wouldn't his congregation be impressed if his son could recite a whole book of the Bible from memory. The Book of Mark was the shortest, so that's the one he chose—not out of any consideration for me, but because he didn't think the congregation would sit still for anything any longer. And I memorized the whole thing."

Andrea looked at him skeptically.

"It's true. I can still recite it all. *The beginning of the Gospel of Jesus Christ,*" he fixed his eyes on some distant point and spoke rapidly in a monotone, " *'the Son of God; as it is written in the prophets, Behold, I send my messenger before thy face, which shall prepare thy way before thee.'* " His manner never once suggested that he took himself seriously, but with a hint of pride, he said, "I can go on if you like. All the way throught to the last Amen."

"No, thanks." Andrea brushed the crumbs from her fingers. "That would probably take an hour or so, wouldn't it?"

"My record is twenty-nine minutes. Of course you don't get a lot of shading or emphasis in a reading like that."

Andrea laughed. "You seem to be a man with a very strange talent. What happened to your illustrious career, anyway?"

"I outgrew being cute. There's nothing very appealing about a clumsy kid with an oversized Adam's apple whose voice is changing. I suffered the fate of a boy soprano."

Andrea turned to get the waiter's attention and ask for the check.

"Let me." Kyle Hagen reached for his billfold. "You've been nice enough to listen to all this foolishness."

"Well, thank you. I really do have to go." She had just noticed Mario Costantino waiting for her near the steps of the

Basilica. "Good luck with your tour directing," she said, leaving a tip. "I suppose you have the guidebook memorized, too."

Hagen allowed that yes, he did. "At least knowing the Book of Mark got me my job and let me spend six months in Venice. The tour company thought throwing in a Bible verse here and there would make my commentary a little more authentic when I herd the tourists through the cathedral. And, like I always say, Andrea, *Why reason ye these things in your heart.*"

Andrea was halfway across the square when she realized she did not know the young man's name. But he knew hers! How could he have known who she was?

Chapter Twelve

Inside the Quadri restaurant, from a table by the window, Georges Tropard watched Kyle Hagen and Andrea in St. Mark's Square. He was certain she was the woman who had tried to get Francesca's attention in the train station. Her reddish hair made her easy to identify. Moreover, he realized he knew her. At least he knew who she was. He was sure he had seen her photograph in art magazines.

While Andrea was standing to leave, Tropard finished his cappuccino and paid the waiter. On his way out, he used his reflection in the beveled glass of the front door to smooth down his scarf and to give himself a self-congratulatory nod. Mademoiselle Perkins could be very useful to his project.

Hagen was so absorbed in a newspaper he had taken from the empty table next to his that he did not know Tropard had walked up beside him until the other man spoke.

"You did not think it was necessary to follow the young lady?" Tropard sat in the chair that Andrea had vacated.

"No. She doesn't suspect anything." Uncharacteristic

worry lines creased Hagen's forehead. "Is everything all right with Francesca and the little girl?"

"They are probably having breakfast on the veranda this very moment."

Hagen did not look less worried as he folded the newspaper and pointed to an article. "Have you seen this? A female body was found last night in a canal near the maritime station."

"I read the newspaper before I left the hotel this morning. May I point out that it says 'an *unidentified* female body.'" Tropard took sunglasses from his pocket and polished them with a white handkerchief. "Something that disagreeable is fairly rare in Venice these days but certainly not in the overall history of the city. I suppose the number of bodies floating in the canal reached its peak during the marauding days of Attila the Hun."

"For God's sake, Tropard, was it the old nun?"

Tropard shook his head sadly. "Yes, I'd say it's very likely."

"You never mentioned murder." Hagen was shocked and angry. "I thought she was going to be kept locked up someplace until we were finished."

"That was the plan. Unfortunately she regained consciousness before the train reached Venice, and she proved stronger and more vocal than they ever would have guessed. Our people panicked, I'm afraid."

"I thought you were such a smooth operator." Hagen was visibly shaken. "It won't take the police long to find out who she was. A missing nun should be fairly easy to trace."

"There was nothing to identify her as a nun. She and her clothing were disposed of separately. And it's unlikely that anyone knows yet that she's missing. Still, it does make time a more important factor than before. We must be finished and on our way by tonight."

"Look, Tropard, theft is one thing, but—"

"My dear Monsieur Hagen, the pleasant evenings spent making plans over brandy are finished. And so is your opportunity for second thoughts." Putting on his dark glasses, Tropard turned his face upward to catch the morning rays of the sun. "Now, tell me what you learned about the young American lady who was with you a few minutes ago."

Hagen turned away. For a moment he was too upset to speak. Then, almost inaudibly, he said, "Her name is Andrea Perkins. She's from Boston, but she came here from Florence. There was nothing special about her train trip, and she's here on business. She knows Costantino, because he was waiting for her at the Basilica and they went off together toward that building behind the church."

"Her name is Andrea Perkins, as you say, but then I told you that last night." Tropard took off his glasses and looked steadily at Hagen. "She is the assistant curator of the Galleria dell' Accademia in Florence. Her specialty is restoration of Italian Renaissance art, but she also is a respected authenticator of art objects."

Tropard enjoyed Hagen's surprised expression. "Her presence here may be very useful to us," Tropard continued. "One of the conditions for payment once the Egyptian bronze is delivered in Paris is that it be, without question, the genuine article. Mademoiselle Perkins' official stamp of approval would be very persuasive if my client should have any questions. Therefore, I suggest that you find out what business she has with Costantino."

"All right. I'll see this through," Hagen said. "But I don't like what happened to that old woman."

"Nor do I. It was a stupid act by witless thugs."

"That may be." Hagen unhooked his umbrella from the back of the chair. "Just don't get any ideas about turning your thugs loose on me."

"My dear friend, how absurd that you should think of

such a thing." Tropard's voice was scolding, then stern. "This is no time for mistrust. We have work to do."

"All I'm saying is, *take heed.*" Hagen grinned. "*With what measure ye mete, it shall be measured to you.*" He turned and walked in the direction of the Basilica.

Tropard replaced his dark glasses and once again turned his face to the sun. He thought, as he had on previous occasions, that he had a lot in common with an aerialist he had once seen at the Comédie Française. There were similarities between his profession as an art thief and a dazzling trapeze artist who spun around in the air and left his audience asking, "How did he do that?"

Naturally, an expert performer did not just climb a ladder and leap into space with no thought of a safety net below. And he needed assistants to make sure the swinging bar was always within his reach. Francesca and Hagen had taken those roles. Now, they were where he needed them: poised at the top of the ladder on their precarious platforms. Before they could even think of how to get back down, he would have reached the ground and taken the net with him. Once he had the bronze mask, Tropard would leave his two young associates to scramble to safety on their own.

In Florence, at about the same time, Aldo Balzani parked his three-year-old Fiat at the Bovio Cleaners. Inside, at the front desk, he talked briefly to the clerk, then went through the double swinging doors to the workroom in back.

"Is your name Stefano?" Balzani had to shout to make himself heard over the hissing steam and the clank of a foot pedal on the mangle operated by a stoop-shouldered man wearing a radio headset.

"Why?" The presser pulled down the earphones and left them whispering around his neck.

Balzani introduced himself, then showed his badge.

"The girl out front said your name is Stefano. Somebody by that name called the police station and said they had seen the makeup girl who disappeared from the Maggio Musicale. Was that you?"

"The manager's not in yet, but I would not want him to know that I called the police."

Balzani shrugged. "I can't think of any reason why he should know who made the call."

"I heard about the shooting on the radio some time ago. It's been a month or two, hasn't it?"

Balzani nodded.

"I remembered, because I thought I knew who the girl was when I first heard her description. They called her the makeup girl on the news—and I suppose she was. But she must have been a sort of assistant, too. She used to bring costumes in here to be cleaned. The manager was always clowning around with her." Stefano took a quick look at the back door and then at the manager's office before he continued.

"For the last six months I am always the first in the shop because I have a new *motocicletta*," he said with a small amount of pride, "and I like to get here before someone else takes the parking space outside the back window. From here, I can see that it is not disturbed during the day. Well, yesterday morning I brought in a container of coffee and was sitting in the corner on a stool behind a big clothes hamper when I saw the makeup girl come in through the front. Right behind her is the manager. They didn't know I was here. Anyway, they both seemed nervous. The manager began to look through a rack of clothes that were ready to be delivered." Stefano paused and asked, "There will be no need to use my name in any of this, will there?"

"I'll tell your boss it was an anonymous tip," Balzani said.

"Well, finally the manager took down a long dress from

the rack and handed it to her. She held it up to her shoulders as though she were trying to see if it was the right size. She shook her head and handed it back to him. He took down another one, and this time it must have been what she was looking for, because they went in his office and he put the dress in a garment box for her. Then she left." The presser started the foot pedal again and began to feed a flowered drape through the mangle.

Balzani watched the procedure for a few seconds then asked, "Is that it?"

"That's all I saw."

"Do you happen to know where she went when she left? Was she in a car? Was she on foot?"

"I don't know. She went back out the front way."

"What did the dress she took look like?"

"I couldn't see it when she was in here. But later in the morning I went over to the rack where the manager had gotten it and that was the interesting part." The dry-cleaning operator folded the drape lengthwise, then attached it with safety pins to a hanger. "You see, we do the work for several churches and schools. Everything else that was hanging on that rack was tagged for the Collegiata Church. What he gave her was a nun's habit."

Balzani thanked the presser and left.

At the front desk, when he asked the cashier, she informed him that the manager was not expected in until midafternoon. It was not possible to reach him at home, she said, because he was visiting his mother in Empoli. This last bit of information was accompanied by raised eyebrows and a greasy-lipstick smirk.

From his car radio, Balzani called his second in command at the police station and told him about the statement from the presser at the Bovio Dry Cleaners. He also gave him a sketchy report of the early-morning telephone conversation with Georgio Conti and asked him to contact the Brufanti Olive Company about the barrel that had been fished from the canal. Before checking in at his office, Balzani made one more stop. He paid a visit to his wounded detective at the Santa Maria Nuova Hospital.

He did not stay long. As he left, he stood outside on the steps, breathing deeply.

Exhaust fumes from the traffic, the stench of a passing garbage truck, and the odor of horse manure in the flower beds at the front of the building were all preferable to the antiseptic smell on the other side the door. He hated hospitals. To him, there was nothing hopeful or reassuring about the gleaming floors, the confident words of the doctors, or the retractable smiles of the nurses. No matter how perfectly squared the sheets were at the corners of the bed occupied by Balzani's detective, the legs beneath the cheerful yellow coverlet still did not move. They never would again. The bullet that had entered the police officer's back at the Maggio Musicale had severed his spine.

When he reached his office, there were three telephone messages on the spindle at the corner of Balzani's desk. The first was a request that he be guest speaker at a civic service club. The second was an invitation to meet for drinks with an old football teammate from Tulane who was in Florence, the note said, on a package tour with a group of fellow dentists. Balzani winced, and then laughed out loud at the thought of the former left guard pulling an unsuspecting patient's teeth. The third message was from Georgio Conti, requesting that Balzani call as soon as he arrived at the office.

In the center of the desk was a report from his assistant on a telephone conversation with an official at the Brufanti Olive Company.

Still standing, Balzani carefully read through the report. When he had finished, he dialed the Venice police station. As he waited to be connected with the captain, he dropped heavily into his battered swivel chair and propped his feet on the open desk drawer.

Georgio Conti coughed and cleared his throat loudly before he answered.

"This is Balzani. How can I help you, Georgio?"

"You could help me a lot if you know how to cure a cold."

"Sorry, I don't diagnose over the phone."

"I'd be fine if I could just get out of this damn place."

"What's wrong with Venice? Don't you like romance?"

"Romance? Who can think of romance when he's coughing and sneezing all the time?" To illustrate, Conti coughed into the phone again. "It's all this blasted humidity. I'm dripping all the time. Haven't had dry feet in two years."

"Maybe it's time you changed your socks."

"Very funny. You're no help."

"I'll try to be if you'll tell me what you wanted to talk to me about."

"Your man up there called me after he checked with the Brufanti Company."

"I just read his report."

"The manager out there said they had a truck stolen yesterday, and that barrel—the one we found the woman in—was on it."

"It says here," Balzani read from the report, "that they found the truck outside the gate this morning, banged in on one side and—with one missing barrel."

"That's right. The barrel was in Florence yesterday," Conti said. "Then it turns up in a canal in Venice early this morning."

"And since Brufanti does all their shipping by rail, the body must have been put in the barrel on the train."

"I thought of that," Conti said.

"So?"

"So, at least we know where the murder was committed."

"On the train."

"That's right. I went over to the freight yard and checked. One of the cars had blood stains on the floor. And wood shavings—as if someone had drilled holes in a barrel."

"Any clothes or personal effects?"

"No." Conti took time out for another rasping cough. "We did fish something else out of the canal that may or may not be related."

"What's that?"

"I've seen hundreds of them just like it in stores that specialize in that sort of thing. You know, places that sell pictures of the Madonna and wall plaques of the Crucifixion. It wasn't fancy, just made out of wood and strung on cotton string. I suppose that's why it floated on the surface."

"What are you talking about, Georgio?"

"A rosary. Normally, it wouldn't even have been turned in to us. It wasn't valuable. But the guy who found it was a sailor in a rowboat from the maritime station. The whole fleet's turned into detectives over there since they found that body. And since the rosary was seen floating in the canal that runs between the freight yard and the dock—near where the barrel was found—the sailor brought it into the station. I'm getting an order to drag the area. Maybe the rest of her clothes are there somewhere."

Balzani let his feet bang on the floor and sat upright in his chair. "Have you got a fix on the age of that dead woman, yet?"

"Not yet."

"What's your guess?"

"I didn't see her. The report says fiftyish—maybe older. But she'd been in the water for a while. They don't look very pretty after that. I wouldn't want to say how old she was until we get something official."

The nun's habit stolen from the Bovio Dry Cleaners and the rosary would link together nicely if it weren't for the matter of age, Balzani thought. It would not be hard to believe that the thief of the pen-and-bister drawing had decided that he no longer needed an accomplice.

Balzani would have sworn, though, that the woman at the Maggio Musicale looked younger than the one Conti had described. In her twenties, he had thought. But he had only seen her for a few seconds as she was running out the door. Maybe he was wrong. Maybe Conti was wrong.

"The interesting thing about the wooden beads," Conti said, "is that they were light-colored raw wood. No shellac or varnish. But some of them had irregular stains. I'm having them analyzed. Could be blood."

Francesca Pelligrino nervously fingered the black-lacquered rosary that Tropard had bought for her to wear with the nun's habit from the Bovio Dry Cleaners.

She sat on the edge of one of the twin beds and watched the sleeping child in the other.

The breathing and pulse of Connie Gilbert's granddaughter seemed normal, but she was taking such a long time to wake up.

Francesca opened the inside shutters and purposely let them bang against the wall.

Mary Louise moaned softly and turned facing the window. Frowning at the light, she put a hand up to shield her eyes before opening them. She lay still, studying Francesca for a long moment before she spoke. "Who are you?"

"I'm Sister Angelica."

"Another one?"

"Yes." Francesca laughed in relief. The child seemed perfectly fine.

"Where's the Sister Angelica that was on the train?"

Francesca was ready with her explanation. She started speaking in Italian then switched to the limited English she learned at school and practiced with members of the American Opera Company at the Maggio Musicale. It had been arranged, she said, by the Scuola per Bambini, for the old nun to travel as far as Venice with Mary Louise. From there, the other Sister Angelica went on to the Lido to visit her brother. "The school sent me to take her place. Now, what would you like for breakfast? And when you're finished, your granddmother says it's all right if we take the vaporetto tour through the canals. Would you like that?"

"I guess." Mary Louise made it a rule not to show too much enthusiasm over anything. In truth, the boats were the *only* thing she liked about Venice. The buildings all looked as though they would crumble down around you and the streets and bridges were too narrow. The vaporetto, though, was all right. The gondolas were better, and the motor cruisers were better still.

"Get dressed, then." Francesca playfully tossed the pillow from her bed at the child. "You're a lazy girl."

Mary Louise giggled. This nun did not seem half bad. At least she *tried* to speak English.

Chapter Thirteen

Mario Costantino waited near the west door of the Basilica for Andrea. He had seen her wave to him when she left the small table in front of Quadri's, where she had been chatting with Hagen. As he watched her walk across the piazza, her white skirt swam with her stride and the sunlight shifted rhythmically across her breasts in the green blouse. Form, color, and youth in such a pleasant combination, Costantino thought: lovely—very pleasant indeed.

With no more than passing curiosity, he wondered what she and that nuisance Kyle Hagen had to talk about? Costantino no longer worried about Hagen, who had not tried to force a meeting in some time. Apparently, he had given up. He could still be seen carrying his red, white, and blue umbrella like a flag, leading his groups of tourists around the square. But the season was almost over. Perhaps he was leaving Venice. It was possible, Costantino thought, that there had never been anything to be concerned about.

What did it matter if Hagen had known Connie Gilbert's daughter in California? That meant nothing. Even if Hagen had succeeded in meeting with Connie, it probably would not have mattered. Whatever Hagen said—whatever dying statement Sandra was supposed to have made—Connie would not have believed him, not when it would have been Hagen's word against Mario's.

Costantino was glad that Andrea had so far to walk across the large piazza. The white skirt and green blouse and the golden tones of bare arms and legs moving toward him was lovely to see. Suddenly Mario turned away, not wanting her to notice that he had been staring. Instead, he watched the guard at St. Mark's, whose job it was to inspect the attire of tourists waiting to enter the Basilica.

There was no escaping the contrast, Costantino thought, between his own view of women and that of the old beadle of St. Mark's. The beadle, in his cocked hat, his suit of eighteenth-century style, and his buckled shoes, clutched a metal staff like the flaming sword of an avenging angel. As the enforcer of the dress code, his frown implied that he would cut down any female who tried to get past him wearing shorts or with bare shoulders or an uncovered head. Mario could not understand the pleasure the old man took in chastising the visitors for their lack of modesty.

Mario was offended only by unattractive bodies. Bulging fat and wrinkled skin were repulsive. But of all the pleasures of man, watching a lovely young woman was second only to touching her.

For many years he had blamed his artist's eye for his fascination with young female bodies. But as he grew older, he admitted to himself that his thoughts were too much of the flesh. He would not concede that he was obsessive—that he was a thoroughgoing voluptuary—but, yes, the silkiness of firm young skin was too often in his thoughts.

Andrea sidestepped a young couple pushing a peram-
bulator and hurried toward the steps of the Basilica. "Mario,
how nice to see you."

"My pleasure." He took her outstretched hand in both of
his and kissed the first knuckle with parted lips. Reluctantly
relasing his hold, he guided Andrea—now with a hand at the
elbow, now with fingers touching her back—around the
corner of the cathedral and through a gate in the wall.

To one side of the enclosed courtyard was a rarity for
Venice, a new building. It was the size of a small warehouse
and had that appearance.

"This is where we will begin our work," Mario said.
"Later we will progress from here to more pleasant surround-
ings inside the Basilica."

Mario unlocked the outer door and preceded her
through the small office. He nodded to a uniformed policeman, who sat leafing through an outdated Italian edition of
Sports Illustrated. A motherly-looking secretary glanced up
from her typewriter and smiled at Mario.

Unlocking a second door, Costantino stood back for
Andrea to enter, then let the door glide closed behind
them.

This inner room was like a safety-deposit vault in a bank.
The walls were lined with locked metal compartments of
various sizes. The larger compartments—with doors about
three feet square—were on the bottom. At the top—eye level
for Andrea—was a row of six-inch doors. Above her head on
two walls were rectangular windows that pushed out and were
held open by metal fulcrums. In the center of the room was a
long wooden work table. Andrea set her canvas tote bag there
and held it open, looking for a notepad and pen.

"Most people think of Venice as having more works of
art per square foot than any other city in the world," Mario
said, reaching in his pocket for a bulging key case. "Unfor-

tunately, only about four percent of the original total is still here."

"How can that be true?" Andrea's eyebrows rose in surprise. "The Palace of the Doge, the cathedral—they're jammed with mosaics and tapestries and . . ."

"We still have a goodly amount, but the nineteenth century was a disaster for Venice. First there was Napoleon, who carted off great quantities of treasure. Then the Austrian occupying forces took their share. Finally, the poor Venetians themselves sold many personal assets to pay for food and fuel."

After disengaging a master key from all the others he carried, Mario unlocked three compartments in the middle row. "What is left, we plan to protect, restore—where needed—and catalog. We've already made some headway. The biggest difficulty is probably a matter of priorities. For centuries, Venetians have not only collected art but religious relics." He began pulling the drawers open one after the other. "You might find this interesting."

When Andrea looked down, she swallowed quickly and stepped back, bumping against Mario. All three boxes were lined with black velvet. In the first, packed in cotton, was an ancient skull with part of the jawbone missing. The second contained the attached bones of an arm and hand, with long curving fingers. In the third was the rib cage of a skeleton.

"I should have warned you," Mario said softly, his mouth next to her ear. There was plenty of room for him to step back and walk around her, but instead, he gripped her by the shoulders then ran his hands lightly down her bare arms before stepping away and closing the compartments.

In an impersonal voice that negated his familiarity of the moment before, Mario said, "Those were saintly bones. Obscure saints, to be sure, but treasured and preserved for centuries by the church. Most of the compartments on this side of the wall are filled with similar relics. The acquisition of the body of Saint Mark was only the beginning of an amazing collection of sainted earthly remains."

Andrea felt flustered and moved back to the table to retrieve her notepad and pen. It was not just the unexpected sight of human bones that bothered her; she was surprised by Mario. Though he was pretending now it never happened, he had made an unmistakable pass. That was what it was: throaty voice, breath on the neck, hands down the arms. She had not counted on having to dodge out of his reach as they worked and was annoyed by the prospect.

"As you know, the body of Saint Mark is now safely encased in granite behind the rood screen in the Basilica. But we have all these other saints and no decision has yet been made as to what should be done with them. There was a time, whenever the Venetian fleet went out, that it returned with a new set of relics. I saw an accounting compiled in fifteen-nineteen that lists fifty-five complete bodies in addition to an incredible number of heads, arms, and fingers. There are not so many now as there once were. Fire destroyed some of them. It almost reached Saint Mark himself in the later part of the tenth century, when the original cathedral burned."

Mario opened another compartment and took out a charred piece of wood about the size of a baseball bat. He handled it with great care, holding it in both hands through the black velvet on which it had rested in the vault.

"This piece of wood," he said, "is believed to be all that remains of a plank that stood between the body of Saint Mark and the fire. It was a part of the lid of the casket." Mario returned the blackened board to the compartment and moved down the room to another section in the vault.

At one of the high windows at the top of the room there

111

was a sudden noise as though something had bumped against the glass.

When Andrea looked up, she had the impression of something darting away. "What was that?"

Mario followed her gaze, but apparently had neither seen nor heard anything.

"Probably a pigeon." He dismissed the incident.

After a pause, Mario continued. "The remains of the saints will not be your concern. But what we hope to establish is the identifcation of everything else in this room. The place of origin . . . age . . . and any other information you can help us find."

He unlocked one of the small compartments on the top row and removed a four-inch bronze cross. Holding it gingerly on its black velvet cushion, he brought it to the table where Andrea now sat. "How, for instance, would you go about identifying this?" He placed it in front of her and stood at her side.

Andrea studied the cross without touching it. She did not like exposing an ancient work of art to the oils and salts of her hands. "Bronze is more difficult to date than, for instance, the piece of wood you showed me. Patina is an indication. The first bronzes were made by combining copper and tin, and they started back to their original ore state almost from the moment they were cast. That's where the green color comes from—the oxides that form on the surface. But I've seen some wonderful fakes." Andrea was warming to her subject and leaned forward to examine more closely the cross with its ridges of varigated green.

"An old farmer who lived near Carrara," she said, "brought a bronze bowl into the Accademia that he said was found buried near the site where Michelangelo quarried his white marble. He told a beautiful story of how it must have belonged to the aritst himself. As it turned out," Andrea laughed, "the man was a pig farmer and had buried the bowl—along with several other modern bronzes—in his pigpen. He had discovered by accident that the chemicals in the manure sped up the aging process and created a convincing patina."

Mario's laugh was much too loud and much too close. Andrea moved to the end of the table, where she had left her tote bag. She took a sheet from a sheaf of printed forms she used when analyzing an object, and started to make notes. Then, deciding that she might as well settle the issue at the beginning, she said, "If we're going to work together, Mario, I'll need a little more distance."

"Signorina?" His face was a study in surprise.

"I think you know what I mean."

"I had no intention of offending," he said innocently.

"It's all right." She was sure he had gotten the message. Shifting the conversation back to the reason she was there, she said, "I'll want to take photographs of a lot of these things, and most of the testing can be done in my lab in Florence. I'll just need to take some samples for analysis. If you want that piece of wood dated, for instance, I'll take a sliver and do a carbon-14 test."

"Yes, of course, however you'd like to proceed." He was all business now. "The bronzes will probably be your major challenge." Unlocking one of the larger compartments on the bottom row, he carefully lifted a bronze sculpture—the face of a man—and laid it on a velvet mat in front of Andrea.

It lay with one cheek turned away. Only a third of the original wooden backing that had held the face straight was left. The wood that remained was warped at and charred, as though it had been subjected to both flood and fire.

It was not a work of art. This was not a sculptor's concept

but a craftman's job. Andrea knew at once that it was an actual death mask of a disturbing face. She would not forget the staring eyes or distorted mouth. There was suffering in the face—and wisdom. It seemed to demand some response from her: some commitment.

"This gentleman," Mario said, "has a recorded history, but we're not sure of its accuracy. What do you think of him? Where do you think he came from?"

"I don't like to speculate," she said. "The fragment of the wooden backing should give us an accurate age, and I'll test the bronze for alloys." She ran one finger lightly over the chin. "The smoothness of the metal and the shade of patina suggest an Egyptian smelting, but I wouldn't make a guess from just looking."

A sudden noise outside, like the falling of loose gravel onto stone, made both Mario and Andrea look quickly toward the corner window.

For just an instant, she was sure she caught a glimpse of a face looking in at them.

Mario agreed that he, too, had seen someone; a curious tourist or perhaps a child had climbed the wrought-iron fence to see what was inside the modern building that was hidden away behind the magnificent Byzantine architecture of the cathedral.

Though Mario felt sure it was nothing to be concerned about, he went outside to look.

He could see that it was possible for someone to climb the wrought-iron fence and brace himself against the building to peer into the high window of the vault.

Though the courtyard was now empty, the gate that led into St. Mark's Square was swinging open.

In the square were hundreds of people milling about, none looking more, or less, suspicous than the other.

As Mario turned back and closed the gate behind him, on the nearby steps of the Basilica, a red, white, and blue umbrella was opened and held aloft to summon the tourists who had paid in advance for the morning tour.

The rest of the day Mario's attitude had been one of hurt formality. Andrea was sure he had been testing the territory earlier with the unnecessary touching and the breathing on her neck. She was also sure that he had gotten her message.

Since then, his air of wounded innocence was beginning to wear thin. For that reason, she accepted when he mentioned that his friend, Connie Gilbert, had invited them for cocktails at her villa that afternoon. Signora Gilbert was eager to meet Andrea, Mario had said, and she had a guest from Paris who would like to make her acquaintance.

Though Andrea was not keen on the idea, she thought an informal half hour or so in the presence of other people might help restore a friendly professional relationship between Mario and herself.

"I'd like to call my hotel first to see if there are any messages," she said.

"Of course." Mario indicated the wall phone, then went to the far end of the room, making a great show of not intruding on her privacy.

The switchboard operator informed her that there had been one call.

"Read it to me, please."

"Yes, signorina. The call was placed from Florence about an hour ago," the operator said. Reading flatly she continued. "It says: 'Signorina Perkins, I am leaving for Venice in a few minutes. All things and my Fiat being equal, I should be at your hotel in about three hours. Please rank in order of preference—gondola ride, dinner, or other diversion of your choice. Aldo.' "

Andrea laughed out loud, then thanked the operator.

"If there are any other calls," Andrea said, "I'll be at—" she placed her hand over the phone and called to Mario, "what is Mrs. Gilbert's address?"

"Number One—Rio di San Travaso."

The sunshine had lasted only through the morning, and as Andrea and Mario entered the square, the symbol of Saint Mark, the winged lion on its high pedestal, jutted into an ominous-looking sky.

Once, it had been in Andrea's mind to ask Mario—a native Venetian who should know—how many winged lions there were in St. Mark's Square. In the square alone, for probably no one knew how many there were in the entire city. When Mark became the patron saint of Venice, the winged lion became his symbol and soon was represented everywhere.

The statue on the granite pedestal, with its agate eyes and its paws resting on the Holy Book, was the most prominent of the lions. But other winged brothers were to be found at every turn; represented in metal, stone, bas-relief plaster, and mosaics. They were painted on wall frescoes, on canvas, on wood, and woven in tapestries. Fierce lions, friendly lions, dead lions, great lions, lions with jeweled eyes, lions with closed eyes, lions sitting, sleeping, stalking, standing, stretching. There were lions on the bell tower and above the face of the zodiac clock; lions on stairways and doorways, on windows, on street signs, on garden gates, on flags, medallions, pillars, tombs, flower pots, drinking fountains, and, of course, churches and chapels.

Andrea had once counted thirty-five winged lions at the Doge's palace before giving up. The guard told her there were seventy-five, in all.

However, on the afternoon when she and Mario crossed the square, her thoughts were not on the symbol of the city. She was thinking of Aldo Balzani and a gondola ride through the Grand Canal, dinner at Florian's, and—first in order of preference—other diversions.

Chapter Fourteen

"For years," Connie Gilbert said, "Mario has tried to interest me in Italian Renaissance painting, but I'll stick with my French Impressionists. At least the Impressionists were honest. They didn't even pretend to represent life as it actually was." She used a long, red-lacquered fingernail to fish an olive from the bottom of her martini glass. "Georges knows what I mean."

Andrea glanced at Connie's friend, Georges Tropard, ensconced in a wicker chair next to their hostess on the veranda. The wicker furniture with custom-made cushions of white fabric patterned in sprays of tulips conveyed an elegant casualness. Georges looked as though the chair had been designed for him. And with his suntan and handsome white hair, Andrea thought the word *distingué* must have come into usage to describe Frenchmen like Georges.

"I suppose it's the religious themes that put me off," Connie said.

Mario, the fourth member of their small group, sighed

as though his great and good friend Connie Gilbert were leading them down a familiar path where he knew every rock and bramble. "Connie." He said her name in a tone that clearly meant she should change the subject.

They were seated under an awning on the veranda of Connie Gilbert's villa near the Accademia di Belle Arti. In front of them was the Grand Canal. To the left, opposite the Canale di San Trovaso—a narrow waterway that fed into the main thoroughfare—was a palazzo owned by a British writer of spy novels and his family. Connie's English neighbors spent their summers in Venice but had already closed and shuttered their villa and returned to London, as they did each year when the October mists began to creep in.

Most of the owners of the villas near the Accademia left for the winter. The fine arts museum itself closed except for a few hours each day. But Connie Gilbert stayed on.

For the past three years, Connie had not been outside the villa. A poorly mended broken hip had made walking so painful that she could not manage at all without inching her way along a wall or clinging to a willing arm on which she could lean.

Her face—which at her age could reasonably have been expected to be lined and creased—was smooth and olive-colored. When she was complimented on her beauty, she freely admitted that she was past sixty-five. And to those who she felt could benefit from the information, she recommended the plastic surgeon in Switzerland whose patient she had been on three different occasions.

That afternoon on the veranda, her hair was covered with a cunningly twisted and tied scarf and her slim body was hidden by a loose caftan of white silk shot through with green metallic threads. Her hands were long and slender. With glinting red fingernails and flashing diamond rings, she used her fingers singly, or in concert, to effectively punctuate her speech.

"The French Impressionists painted flowers and dancers, chairs, prostitutes, cafés, themselves, and each other," Connie said. "Things they'd seen—things they knew about. I'm sorry, Mario darling, but when I look at the work of the Renaissance painters—all of it with religious themes, and all of it so boringly beautiful—my heart goes out to the fifteenth-century priests." Connie paused to sip her drink and examine her fingernails, waiting for someone to ask her to explain.

"What is your concern for them?" Georges neatly bridged the gap in her monologue.

"Think of some grubby little priest," she said, "bald, too fat, probably with some teeth missing. And think of the model set up for him by Botticelli and Leonardo and the rest who painted Christ as neat and clean and handsome as a film star. How could my miserable little guy, probably with splotchy skin from scratching at fleas or lice or worse—how could he hope to be Christlike?" She shot a mischievous glance at Andrea, knowing full well that most of her waking hours were spent restoring or evaluating art from the Italian Renaissance and that therefore she presumably had a particular fondness for the period. "What do you think, Andrea?"

What she thought was that Connie enjoyed starting arguments. Andrea liked the wealthy American widow and saw her attempts to be outrageous as a means of entertaining her guests. She appeared to be succeeding, at least with Georges, whom she had introduced as her art dealer from Paris. As such, he could hardly be expected to disagree with his client's views. Mario, however, was becoming annoyed—as much at the number of martinis Connie was drinking, Andrea suspected, as with what she had to say.

"My field is art, not religion," Andrea said evenly. "I don't know much about your priest with the splotchy skin." She eyed her glass of Pinot Bianco and decided that another few minutes was all she need spend to finish her wine and make a polite exit.

It was now late afternoon, but there were no clear-cut slanting shadows to indicate the time of day. A thin fog was draped over the city like gray gauze.

"The point is"—Connie aimed this at Mario, her most vulnerable target—"why did the Renaissance painters always equate spiritual beauty with physical beauty?"

"Who's to say their concept was wrong?" A trace of anger curled the edge of Mario's voice.

"That's what it was—just a concept with no basis in reality. They never saw Christ." Connie smiled triumphantly. "What made them think they knew what he looked like? There were no portraits or photographs to work from. A walk through the Basilica will show you what I mean. Every mosaic, every tapestry, every painting of Christ or the saints is more beautiful than the last . . ."

"What's wrong with that?"

"Oh, Mario, it's all so obvious. It's like the Renaissance boys came along and said, well, what Christ and the saints— Christ and the saints—" Connie's speech was beginning to slur. Overcompensating, she began to pronounce each word with great care. "What Christ and the saints did and said and wrote was pretty good, these guys from the Renaissance thought, but not quite good enough. We can improve on it. We'll make them beautiful to look at."

Mario's hand flew up in an angry gesture. "For God's sake, Connie. Would it make you happier if they were all hunchbacks or cross-eyed?"

"Not all of them." Connie grinned wickedly. "But maybe a few."

122

Georges laughed and Mario looked as though he were about to bite through his wine glass.

"Think of Leonardo's *The Last Supper*, for instance," Connie went on. "Those were all fine-looking men gathered there at the table, all graceful and in spotless robes. If nothing else, don't you wonder who did their laundry?"

Georges laughed again, and Andrea smiled. Mario continued to scowl.

"And the ultimate in conceit," Connie paused to finish her martini, "is a Michelangelo statue I saw in Florence. What's the name of it, Andrea? *Descent from the Cross?*"

"There is a magnificent work by that name. It's one of the unfinished sculptures."

"That's it. Now, I'm not arguing skill or beauty. Skill and beauty don't enter into it. I'm just talking about ego. In that statue, Michelangelo sculpted his own face as Joseph of . . . where was Joseph from?"

"Joseph of Arimathaea," Andrea supplied.

"Arimathaea. Joseph of Arimathaea. In that statue, here was Michelangelo—holding the dead body of Jesus as though he, personally, was going to use his influence with God to see to it that Christ got to heaven. Mario, refill Andrea's glass."

"No, really. I'm going to have to leave soon." Andrea reached toward her briefcase and tote bag.

Not wanting a member of her audience to disappear, Connie said, "Well, Andrea, aren't you going to defend your Renaissance giants?"

"The only help they need from me is to patch up their work and help preserve it." Andrea had no intention of sparring with Connie.

"And the reason it's important to preserve Renaissance art," Mario said with evangelical fervor, "is because for centuries people had admired it and taken inspiration from it. My dear Connie, how inspired do you think the average person would be by a painting in the Basilica, for instance, of your toothless priest scratching his flea bites? It's only natural to be attracted to physical beauty."

"Yes, Mario," Connie said. "I know all about your attraction to physical beauty."

In the wake of Mario's sudden silence, Connie took inventory of the hors d'oeuvres tray and her own glass that was almost empty again, then pulled the bell cord next to the balustrade.

Georges, ever attentive to his hostess, refilled her glass from a crystal martini pitcher on the cocktail table.

"Mario used to paint, you know," Connie said. "I always thought he showed great promise. But he gave it up. The last thing he did was that portrait on the wall behind you, Andrea."

Andrea turned to look.

"That was my daughter. Sandra."

The painting gave the impression of a hand-tinted black and white photograph. The colors were not quite right, but a great deal of effort had gone into portraying the subject exactly as she must have appeared. She was a young woman in her late teens or early twenties with light brown hair, a pouting mouth, and skeptical blue eyes.

Suddenly Connie's voice boomed, "Mary Louise, sweetheart! Come in."

Andrea glanced toward the door to see who the new arrival was. Standing there, holding a tray of marinated mushrooms, was a blond, seven-year-old version of the girl in the portrait.

With a flash of diamonds and fingernails, Connie motioned for the child to come to her. "Darling, meet Miss Perkins and Monsieur Tropard."

Mary Louise, not yet sure that she would allow herself to

124

be drawn into the group, kept to the doorway, where she turned her large blue eyes first on Tropard, then on Andrea. "I already know her," she said, looking steadily at Andrea. She added, "You're the lady from Bloomingdale's."

Connie laughed. "Bloomingdale's?"

"What a nice surprise to see you again." Andrea explained to Connie, "Mary Louise and I met last night on the train from Florence. She pegged me as an American right away by reading my tote bag." For the benefit of the two men, she added, "It says Bloomingdale's on the side."

"I see. Then that's one introduction taken care of." Connie motioned again to the little girl. "Come in and put that down, darling. I want you to meet our other guest. Why are you carrying that tray, anyway? Where is Eleonara? Or Sister Angelica?" Turning toward the doorway Connie called in a husky voice, "Sister Angelica? Are you out there?"

From the shadows beyond the doorway, a soft voice answered. "Yes. But Eleonora has gone, Signora Gilbert. She went home."

"Went home? Without telling me?"

Venturing a few steps onto the veranda, a young woman in a nun's habit said, "She told me she felt ill."

Later, Andrea would realize that she should have suspected something was wrong. The girl Connie Gilbert called Sister Angelica was acting strangely. As soon as the girl spoke she looked at Tropard for—what?—assurance? Approval? They supposedly had never met. Why should the shy little nun from the Scuola per Bambini be concerned with what the worldly Frenchman thought of her behavior?

"If you've met my granddaughter," Connie said to Andrea, continuing with the introductions, "then you must have met Sister Angelica on the train, too." Connie encouraged the young woman to join them. "Come in, my dear."

"We didn't actually meet," Andrea said, smiling. "The last time I saw Sister Angelica, she was carrying a very sleepy little girl through the terminal."

"Mary Louise was still asleep when they got here," Connie said. "It's not like her at all. I was afraid she was sick, but there was no fever. And experience has taught me to be grateful when a six-year-old is asleep."

"Almost seven," Mary Louise said.

Connie gave her granddaughter an indulgent smile. "Sister Angelica, I'd like you to meet Monsieur Tropard."

Tropard rose. "The pleasure is mine."

Mario stood to offer her a chair. Tropard, however, was faster on his feet and pulled out a striaght-back chair from a table near the door.

Not minding that his duty as host had been usurped, Mario sat again and turned his attention to Mary Louise. His face had lit in a smile the moment the little girl appeared. As she walked past him to put the tray on the cocktail table he lightly touched her soft blond curls.

Finishing up the formalities, Connie said, "And, Monsieur Tropard, may I present my granddaughter, Mary Louise."

"*Enchanté, mademoiselle.*" Tropard took the child's hand with a courtly bow. "Did I understand your grandmother to say you do not feel well?"

"I'm okay." Mary Louise took back her hand and hid it behind her. Turning to look at Andrea, she rolled her eyes to show how extremely bored she was.

"Damn that maid for taking off without bothering to check with me." Connie lifted her empty glass. "Mario, dear, would you . . .?"

Mario, whose eyes had scarcely left Mary Louise since she came on the scene, started at the sound of his name.

"Allow me, Madame Connie." Tropard did the honors.

After filling the glass of his hostess, he excused himself, saying he had left something in the hall that he would like to bring in at this time.

Francesca waited until he was gone, then said something about a handkerchief and followed him from the veranda.

"You get prettier every time I see you." Mario reached out and lifted Connie's granddaughter onto his lap. "While you're here, I'll take you to Murano and show you where they make glass the same color of blue as your eyes. Would you like that?"

"I guess," she said with a shrug, then squirmed off his knee and went to renew her acquaintance with Andrea.

Deserted, Mario moved his chair closer to Connie and began speaking to her earnestly in a low voice.

Mary Louise climbed onto the arm of the couch where Andrea sat. In a matter-of-fact tone, she said, "She's not the same one who was on the train."

"Who?" The only person the little girl could have been referring to was the nun. But Andrea simply did not understand.

"Sister Angelica."

Days later, Andrea would realize that she should have seen it all immediately. At least she should have asked the child what she meant. But at the time it happened, Andrea was distracted—and embarrassed—by the whispered conversation between Mario and Connie that had become louder and blossomed into an argument.

"I'm only reminding you that you are drinking too much," Mario said.

"What the hell difference does it make?"

"I'm concerned about you."

"Don't worry, I won't say anything else about Sandra."

". . . and you're talking too loud."

Their voices grew softer again.

Mary Louise, with her foot on the arm of the couch, had begun to unravel a pink flower that was embroidered on her white stocking. She appeared not to have heard Mario and her grandmother. Andrea pretended that she had not.

As soon as Tropard reappeared, Andrea decided, she would leave.

"I like this Sister Angelica better, anyway."

Andrea was not listening to the child. She was mentally rehearsing her exit line as she watched Mary Louise destroy her stocking. Absently, she wondered if she should warn the little girl that pulling the threads out that way would leave a hole. It also crossed her mind that the anger she heard in Connie's voice might be turned on her granddaughter if she saw the little girl sitting with her foot on the upholstered arm of the couch.

". . . keep pouring down those martinis, you'll fall and break your other hip."

"Shh. Now who's talking too loud?"

During that exchange, Mary Louise was saying, "My grandmother said there are so many nuns at that dumb school, it's no wonder I can't keep them straight." The little girl stopped long enough to pull her other foot up, hugging her knees to her chest and digging the heels of both shoes into the white upholstery. "*Then* she asked me if they ever gave us wine for dinner to make us sleep."

Andrea smiled and lightly grasped both the child's ankles in one hand, gently straightening her legs. "You're wearing your new shoes. Aren't these the ones that came from Bloomingdale's?" Letting go of her hold, she let the short legs dangle harmlessly over the arm of the couch.

"You've seen them before," Mary Louise said with the disdain Andrea knew her comment deserved. "I wore them last night on the train."

"Mademoiselle Mary Louise!" Georges Tropard stood in

the doorway holding a flat foil-wrapped box. "Your grandmother had told me that tomorrow is your birthday. In honor of such an occasion, I present this to you."

Andrea saw that she could not leave quite yet. It was only polite to wait until Mary Louise opened her package.

Chapter Fifteen

Kyle Hagen rested one foot on a wooden piling in Connie Gilbert's boat slip as he concluded negotiations with her driver. Above his head on the veranda, he could hear Tropard's voice more distinctly than the other three. Good. Tropard was sitting next to the window that overlooked the Grand Canal, as he had said he would.

Time was growing short, and Hagen was becoming impatient with the boatman. "This is the amount we agreed on." He looked down at the wiry man in the striped shirt beside him and counted out a generous handful of lire.

"Ah, yes. We agreed, but still I worry. What if the boat is damaged?"

"It won't be."

"If I lost my job, what would I do? I am always a boatman. And I have a family . . ."

His argument began to trail off. There were only the two of them standing next to the cruiser *Villa Constance*. Hagen outweighed the little Italian by a good twenty pounds and was an easy six inches taller. There was no real contest. Still, the boatman would not have forgiven himself if he had not attempted to haggle.

In truth, it did not matter if he lost the job. He would renew his union dues and drive a *vaporetto* again. And he was more than satisifed with the amount of money the American and the Frenchman were paying him for the use of Madame Gilbert's boat.

"Lock it to the dock when you return." He handed the keys to Hagen, and started down the narrow walkway to his own small outboard. "There are thieves everywhere in Venice."

The boat dock was the equivalent of a four-car garage. There was the six-seated cruiser, the *Villa Constance*, a moldering gondola that had not been used for years, a small runabout, and an open slip for guest docking.

A carved wooden door at the back of the dock led to what was once the veranda and the entertainment center of the villa. Now it was used for boat repairs and high-shelf storage. As Venice had continued to sink, the residents, over the years, moved their living quarters up to the next floor. Sometimes it had been necessary to add another story.

The boat keys Hagen dropped in his pocket clanked against a room key from the Hamilton Plaza that had been given to him by a friendly TWA Getaway tour director, a blonde named Janice Williams.

Over the summer, Hagen had chalked up a high degree of success with the female tour directors from several different travel agencies and airlines. He had shared a bus seat— and a bed—as the guest of a sultry brunette from Alitalia on a two-day land-package tour to Capri and Pompeii. He had attended an Overnight-in-Arezzo to see the medieval tilting and jousting competition as the guest of another brunette employed by the British Wanderlust agency. Tomorrow morning at seven, he was leaving on the TWA Getaway bus for a Shoppers' Extravaganza in Milan. Janice Williams had handed Hagen her room key and said, "We may as well get an early start on our own extravaganza."

What Janice did not know was that for Hagen it would be a one-way trip. He had his own getaway plans for tomorrow. He had made a reservation on a plane that left Milan's Malpensa airport one hour after the TWA bus was due to arrive. Tropard did not know that, either.

Hagen had learned a lot from Tropard about subtlety in planning and patience. He had also learned not to trust the Frenchman.

Unlocking the padlock that secured the *Villa Constance* to the dock, Hagen jumped behind the steering wheel, ready to back out of the slip as soon as it was necessary.

It will not be me, Hagen thought, who can '*see and not perceive*' . . . and '*hear and not understand.*' He had seen the way Tropard manipulated stupid little Francesca. He had heard the glorious promises the Frenchman had made to her. She would be lucky if she did not wind up like the real nun she replaced.

Nothing like that would happen to Hagen. If the circumstances were right, he might even peddle the Egyptian mask in America.

"It's a panda bear!" Francesca stood in the doorway and watched as Mary Louise spread open the tissue paper in the foil-wrapped box.

"It's charming," Connie Gilbert mumbled behind glittering fingers that wiped across her mouth, slid down her chin, and dropped limply into her lap. She was drunk and no longer even trying to salvage her enunciation.

"For God's sake, Connie," Mario said under his breath.

Connie ignored him. " 'S lovely gift. Thank Monsieur Tropard, darling."

"Thanks." Mary Louise cut her eyes briefly toward Tropard. The black-and-white stuffed animal was almost as large as she was. She lifted it from the box and, with a rare smile, hugged the fuzzy bear. Then solemnly, as though embarrassed, she whispered to Andrea, "I don't really play with stuffed toys much anymore."

"I still like them," Andrea said. She found something touching and a little sad about the child's determination to be self-sufficient.

An instant of quiet that dropped like a sigh in a conversation prompted Andrea to stand and start her good-byes.

"No, Andrea, please." Connie's hands fluttered around her knees. "Stay and entertain these gen'leman. 'Fraid I must lie down for a while . . ."

Mario was immediately at Connie's side, helping her to her feet. It was obvious that she was going to have trouble walking even with his support.

Francesca, as though to shield the child from what might be an embarrassing scene, took Mary Louise by the hand and said, "There's another surprise waiting for you downstairs." Quickly, she led the little girl from the room.

"Mademoiselle Perkins," Tropard said softly. "I would offer to help with Madame Gilbert, but perhaps another woman . . ."

"Of course." Andrea took Connie's other arm. Slowly, the three of them made their way from the veranda, through the foyer to a large bedroom draped with deep green velvet.

"Don' usually get drunk that fast." Connie sat heavily on the edge of an over-sized bed covered with the same plush fabric.

"It's all right, Con," Mario said. "It was that damned

Frenchman. He kept refilling your glass everytime you took a sip."

With a silly giggle, Connie scooted her feet from her shoes. "Enjoyed it, though," she said.

Mario lifted her legs up onto the bed as she fell back against the pillows, then he bent and kissed her forehead.

"We're really a couple of old fools, aren't we, Mario?" She took his hand and held it against her cheek for a moment.

Andrea silently left the room and retraced the route to the veranda. She intended to get her briefcase and tote bag and leave as quickly as possible.

Mario followed her. "I would like to apologize . . ."

"No, I'm sorry she isn't well," Andrea protested.

"With all the excitement of having Mary Louise here . . ."

"Will Mrs. Gilbert be able to manage?"

"Oh, yes. Even if the maid doesn't show up again, Sister Angelica and I can take care of Mary Louise—and Connie."

When Andrea reached the veranda, she looked immediately toward the leg of the couch where she had propped her belongings and was puzzled to see that they were no longer there.

"I borrowed them, Andrea," Tropard said evenly.

He was seated in the chair next to the window where he had been before. Her briefcase was spread open across his knees, and it was obvious that he had been going through the contents.

Without a hint of apology, he held up a crisp sheet of expensive paper he had found inside and asked, "Is this the form you use for authentication?"

Andrea did not answer but stood and stared at him in surprise.

Mario's face flushed with indignation. "You have no right to look through Signorina Perkins' belongings."

Tropard ignored Mario. "It's quite impressive." He read aloud the heading of the document which was written in script. " 'Galleria dell' Accademia, Florence, Italy.' I particularly like the scroll work in gold around the edges. Such a classical Florentine touch."

Andrea wondered angrily if he had planned to steal the documents from her? Surely, though, Tropard was too clever, too smooth to let himself be discovered this way. Then what was he doing with her briefcase? "They're worthless without the seal and my signature," she said.

"A seal, yes. That would enhance the appearance. Do you use wax for the seal? No, I don't suppose wax is used these days." He smiled thoughtfully. "Probably an ink stamp of some sort, or an adhesive paper medallion." Tropard closed the briefcase and handed it to her, still holding the single sheet of paper.

"With this basic form it would be easy enough to fool most of my clients," he said.

"Unless they checked with me."

"Oh, that would never happen." Tropard laughed and casually dropped the ornate vellum sheet into Andrea's open tote bag beside him. "No one would ever see the document but my client. And perhaps a few of his trusted friends."

With no further word, Andrea firmly gripped the briefcase in one hand and picked up the tote bag with the other. Turning her back to Tropard, she said to Mario, "I'll see you at the vault tomorrow morning, then."

"Andrea. Wait a moment," Tropard said.

Automatically she looked in his direction but she was not going to let Tropard detain her any longer. That was her intention until she saw that he was standing, and in his hand—even though it was aimed safely at a corner of the room—was a gun.

Mario had been quietly fuming until now. "What is this

about, Tropard?" Anger visibly spread across Mario's face. He started toward the other man.

"This gun is real," Tropard said. "Sit down. Both of you." His voice was low and convincing.

Andrea sat on the couch. Mario slumped in a chair by the door, his chest heaving, his hands making fists.

"You may as well be calm and listen to what I say. I apologize for the gun. Its only purpose is to get your attention. Once you hear me out, I think we can work together with no problem at all." Tropard sat and crossed his legs, balancing the gun almost casually on his knee. "I have a client who is very eager to own an object that is in the vault behind the Basilica. In a few minutes we will go there and you, Mario, will get it for me. And Mademoiselle Perkins will give me a certificate of authentication—signed, and with a proper seal."

"No, Tropard." Mario laughed and threw his hands out expansively. "It can't be done."

"I am convinced that it can."

"Do you know how many times thieves have tried to rob the Basilica?"

"No. But it's not important."

"Napoleon did it, but he had an army," Mario said. "Where's your army?"

"Perhaps I have one. But if I don't, why do you say it's impossible?"

"First, to get there we'll have to go in a boat." Mario spoke as though he were explaining to a child. "There are police patrols in the canal between here and there. Even if we don't attract their attention in some way, once we get to St. Mark's Square there are people everywhere. How are you going to keep a gun on two of us and herd us through the crowd? And—if we get that far—there is an armed guard outside the building, and one inside."

"Plus, I'm quite sure there is a hidden alarm in the vault that would summon a swarm of policemen," Tropard said. "Am I not right?"

Mario did not answer.

"I would have been surprised if the builder had not included that safeguard."

Andrea asked, "What is it you want from the vault?" She admired Mario's bravado, though she was not convinced.

"I understand that you examined it this afternoon. There is no accounting for taste, but my client is quite eager to own the antique Egyptian death mask."

"No." There was no bluff in Mario's voice this time. "No, I won't leave this building."

"Yes, my friend, you will. And I'll tell you why." Tropard glanced out the window before he continued. "Actually, it is just as well that Madame Gilbert is not here. There is no need to upset her, too."

For a moment, Andrea wondered if Tropard had drugged Connie. But, no, he must have known that all he had to do to get her out of the way was to keep her martini glass filled.

"A few weeks ago," Tropard said, "I made the acquaintance of a young man who met Madame Gilbert's daughter, Sandra, in California. The story she told him—and which he has told me—is an interesting one."

Mario glared at the Frenchman, who seemed not to notice.

"It concerned a summer several years ago here at her mother's villa. Sandra was young, seventeen or so, I think. The age doesn't matter. She was past the age of consent—at least in my country. If you will forgive a rather indelicate comment, she had already consented more than once before the summer in question."

Mario had shifted his gaze to the floor and his shoulders were slumped.

"That summer while she was here, her mother's lover—you, my dear Mario, were inspired to take up your long-neglected paints and create a portrait of this child. Young woman, rather. She had *been* a child when she last went away to school. But over the year, like little girls will, she changed. She became a desirable young woman.

"It is not unknown, Monsieur Costantino, that you have a fondness for pretty girls. A waitress at Quadri's laughed about your attentions to her. And a manicurist who works in the same building as yours volunteered, when I inquired about you, that as she shaped the nails on one of your hands, she kept her eyes on your other one."

"Shut your filthy mouth, Tropard."

"You're only human, my friend. I envy your good fortune. For a whole summer an agreeable and *willing* young girl lived in the same house with you."

Andrea had been watching Mario. His head was down, and she could not see his face clearly, but when he rubbed at his eyes with the flat of his hand, she protested. "Tropard. Surely this isn't necessary."

"Yes, I'm afraid it is. But I won't prolong the story. As often happens, a choice had to be made. Sandra wanted you to go back to America with her, didn't she, Mario?"

Mario did not answer.

"The fact that you chose the mother instead of the daughter—for whatever reason—may have had nothing to do with Sandra's death. There were other factors, too. She got in with an unsavory group in California, which is why Connie has custody of petite Mary Louise. After that, Sandra made an effort to reform, so to speak. She joined an obscure church group headed up by a Reverend Hagen, the father of Kyle

Hagen—whom you have successfully avoided this summer. But, alas, religion was not the answer for her. The fact is, she wasted the rest of her short life and ended it with a bullet."

"Your friend Hagen tried to blackmail me," Mario said in a choked voice. "He wasn't successful, and you won't be, either. Connie wouldn't believe your story about Sandra and me even if you told her. Because she doesn't want to."

Tropard looked out the window for a moment. "This is such a lovely time of afternoon in Venice. The sun is out. Had you noticed? Come to the window, both of you. There is something I want you to see."

Neither Andrea nor Mario moved.

"If you are wondering, either of you, what I would do if you tried to leave this room," Tropard said wearily, "I'd shoot you." He motioned with the gun for them to join him at the window.

Andrea believed what he said.

Mario looked as though he were going to defy Tropard, but something—Andrea suspected it was curiosity— brought him to the window, too.

Under other circumstances Andrea would have agreed that she had seldom seen the Grand Canal look lovelier. It was like a Canaletto painting. A few gondolas glided on the sparkling surface, a vaporetto hurried by, a canopied cabin cruiser speeded toward the wide basin in the direction of the Lido.

The Grand Canal was at its widest here. Connie's villa was near the point where the canal emptied into St. Mark's basin, which was wider still. The boats seemed to preen in the uncommon space around them and gave each other a wide berth which was never possible during the peak summer season nor even in winter during the busy mornings.

As Andrea and Mario watched, Tropard with one hand unknotted the silk scarf around his neck and waved it out the window. A motor started below, and there was the sound of water sloshing against the dock. Suddenly, beneath them, the *Villa Constance* came into view, backing out of the boat slip beneath Connie Gilbert's veranda. It was moving fast and in a short time was near the center of the canal. When it appeared that the boat was as far from one shore as the other, the driver cut the motor to its lowest speed, then shifted to idle. The *Villa Constance* bobbed and drifted in the gentle wake of other distant boats.

The watchers at the window could clearly see the four who were on board. The man at the wheel wore a gondolier's hat that shaded his face. In the seats behind him were a woman in nun's garb, a small blond girl, and a large toy panda.

"Now watch closely," Tropard said.

The driver took off his hat and dropped it beside him. From the seat he took a closed red, white, and blue umbrella and waved it toward the villa.

"Good God. That's Kyle Hagen!" Mario's first reaction was not fear, but complete astonishment at seeing Hagen in Connie's boat.

"Keep watching," Tropard demanded.

The woman dressed as a nun stood, swaying with the motion of the water. She reached to the top of her head and unhooked the black woolen veil, holding it aloft and letting it flutter in the wind. Then, she rolled it in a ball and dropped it on the seat. The breeze caught her long dark hair and lifted it above her head as she removed the white wimple that framed her face and the yoke about her neck and shoulders.

Dressed only in black, with one hand now resting on the top of the child's head, the other upraised to the tangle of dark hair that swirled wildly about her face in the breeze, she looked like a creature from Neptune's kingdom.

Though Andrea still did not fully understand, dread

weakened her knees and turned her hands clammy. Mario had grown pale and was gripping the window ledge.

"As you see, there's no danger yet," Tropard said. He dropped the gun casually into his pocket. "But, Monsieur Costantino, until I have the Egyptian mask, your young daughter will not be back on shore."

Chapter Sixteen

Watching the *Villa Constance* drift peacefully in the canal, it was hard for Andrea to imagine that such a quiet scene could evoke such a feeling of horror.

"As you have guessed, good Sister Angelica is not what she appeared to be." Tropard helped himself to a glass of Pinot Bianco from Connie Gilbert's cocktail table and sat with his back to the window. "She is neither quiet as a nun, chaste as a nun, nor has she received the vows of a nun. She is merely an agreeable young woman I brought with me to help persuade you to cooperate, Monsieur Costantino."

Andrea put a hand on Mario's arm. He was rigid. For a moment, he could not look away from the three people drifting in the boat out toward the basin, out toward the Lido, out toward the Gulf of Venice.

"Sandra's child—*your* child—is not in danger at the moment. Certainly *she* has no fear. Francesca's behavior with the headgear may be puzzling to her, but a seven-year-old is more accepting of aberrant behavior than we adults are." Tropard smiled eerily.

"Consider the possibilities," he said. "The boat is quite fast, I understand. It may be that Monsieur Hagen and I have arranged to take petite Mary Louise to the Lido and hide her there until you decide to cooperate. Of course the Lido is only one of many possibilities among the islands of Venice." Tropard laid the gun down on the cocktail table as though he had no further need for it.

Andrea thought of running to Connie's room and barricading the door. Would there be time to call the police before Tropard came after her? It was possible. But it was also possible that he could signal the boat and send it into hiding before the police arrived.

"Or it could be," Tropard continued, "that nothing as prolonged as a kidnapping would suit my purposes. I am, after all, eager to get back to Paris. With that in mind, something of a more immediate nature would be more practical. So, I ask you to consider the possibility that the panda bear has a timing device with explosives and that I have a remote control mechanism in my pocket. I'll confide in you, Monsieur Costantino, I share your dislike for Hagen. And I have no particular fondness for Francesca."

Hoping to reassure Mario, Andrea said, "That's absurd, Tropard. You're not a terrorist." But she was convinced that he was a coldly dangerous man who would follow up on whatever threat he made. "What could you possibly gain by blowing up the boat?"

"It would not be my choice to do that. All I wish to do is collect the Egyptian mask and deliver it to my client."

"If you harm that child," Mario's voice was strained and husky, "I'll kill you, Tropard."

Tropard laughed. "You forget, monsieur, I am the one with the gun." He smiled genially at them both. "But even if there is no bomb, it is possible that the child would fall overboard."

"There would be witnesses," Andrea protested. "Other boats are out there."

"Yes, but notice that none are close enough to see how such an accident would happen." Tropard glanced out the window for the first time in several minutes. "And who would suspect a nun of complicity in such a tragic event?"

Andrea saw that the girl Tropard called Francesca was wearing the yoke, wimple, and veil again.

The sun was fading. It still glimmered in shifting patterns across the water, but it would be gone soon, Andrea thought. Then what would happen? When there was no more daylight they would not be able to see Mary Louise. They would not know for sure that she was still unharmed.

Boats, a half-dozen or so, moved in an unhurried way in the canal. As Andrea watched, a small motorcraft pulled beside the idling *Villa Constance*. The driver exchanged some words with Hagen. Andrea imagined that the stranger was asking if the stalled cruiser was in trouble? The smaller boat must be offering help. Her heart sank when she saw Hagen wave him off with some explanation. The other boatman good-naturedly waved back and headed toward St. Mark's Square.

Mario at last turned away from the window and faced Tropard. "What do you want me to do?"

"It's quite simple." Tropard put down his wineglass and loosely tied the scarf around his neck, pocketing the gun again.

"You two will precede me down the stairs to the dock where we will board Madame Gilbert's small motorboat." It was as though he were hosting a sight-seeing tour. "And Mademoiselle Perkins," he said as though he were reminding her to wear a jacket, "don't forget your briefcase."

Mario led the way. As Andrea followed, she thought, if only it were an hour later, Aldo Balzani would be here. What would he do in this situation? She could think of nothing that Tropard had not already anticipated. There seemed no choice but to do as he asked. It was not as though the danger were Andrea's own. She would have considered taking risks if that were the case. She would have looked for a weapon—a docking chain or rope, a metal oar—something to use to get Tropard off balance. He did not even have the gun in his hand. He had put it in his pocket. But anything she did would increase the danger for the child in the boat.

If Balzani had left Florence at the time she calculated from his message, he was still on the *autostrada*.

She had given Connie's address to the desk clerk at the Hamilton Plaza just in case Balzani arrived early. That was unlikely—not in his Fiat. But if he did, and he tried to telephone the villa, would Connie answer? Probably not. It would take more than a ringing telephone to wake her and there was no one else in the house.

Suppose Balzani came directly to the villa without calling. Was there some way she could leave him a message? How could she let him know something was wrong?

"Monsieur Costantino," Tropard said when they were near the bottom of the stairs, "you will drive us to the dock on the west side of the Basilica."

"What about the *Villa Constance*?"

"Your daughter will be safe for the time being."

"How do I know that?"

"You'll be able to see for yourself. They will follow us." Tropard smiled. His hand was on the gun in his pocket. "It's a concession I made to Monsieur Hagen, who has a suspicious mind. It occurred to him that I might not return to the villa once you had gotten the mask from the vault for me. This way—traveling in a sort of caravan—we'll be able to watch each other."

"Will he bring Mary Louise to shore as soon as we've left the vault?"

"No." Tropard reached for Andrea's briefcase and put it on the floor of the boat. "You were quite right, Monsieur Costantino, about mingling with so many people in St. Mark's Square. A delicate exchange such as this requires privacy. We will come back here to conclude our business."

Andrea hung back near the bottom of the stairs. The two men were busy with the lock on the chain that secured the boat to the dock. Waiting for a moment when Tropard was turned away, she set her tote bag in the center of the bottom step. Because of the banister it could not be seen from the dock. But if Balzani came for her it would be the first thing he saw when he started up the stairs. He would know something was wrong if she left her precious bag of art supplies behind.

Mario was still obviously shaken. He fumbled with the keys. Tropard took them from him and with a steady hand released the lock and the chain.

"What proof do I have," Mario asked, "that you will bring Mary Louise back at all?"

"None," Tropard said lightly. Then seeing that Mario's nervousness could lead to a reckless blunder, he said reassuringly, "Over there is evidence of our intention to return." He nodded toward a wooden bench. Folded neatly on top were blue jeans and a woman's sweater. Beside them, were a man's knit shirt and a corduroy jacket. "Francesca and Hagen are coming back here to change. Their own clothing will attract less attention than their present attire of a gondolier and a nun. You see, we are even reconciled to the fact that you will alert the police once we've gone." Unhooking the boat from the chain, he turned to Andrea. "You will get in the back, please, Mademoiselle Perkins."

Andrea did as he ordered.

"Let's get on with this, Tropard. It'll be dark soon," Mario said. "If anything happens to that child . . ."

"You must be calm, Monsieur Costantino. We all wish to complete our project as quickly as possible." He stepped aside for Mario to get in the boat. "You will be our driver."

When Mario was seated behind the wheel, Tropard climbed in beside him.

The motor coughed and sputtered as Mario turned the key. "This boat hasn't been used in several days." He tried again. It caught and held. Hurriedly, he began backing out. The boat bumped against a red-and-white striped pole that marked the exit.

"Not so fast," Tropard said. "We don't want a patrol boat to cite us for speeding."

All that remained of the earlier sunshine was a fading streak of gold on the horizon. Even that was quickly giving way to an encroaching fog that seemed to both rise from the water and descend from the sky.

Only a few other boats were anywhere nearby in the canal.

A large tanker making its way toward the gulf had already turned on its lights in the growing darkness.

Tropard unfastened his scarf again and waved it as a signal for the *Villa Constance* to follow. Hagen raised a hand in response.

Mary Louise saw the smaller boat leave her grandmother's dock. Before Francesca could stop her, the little girl stood in the seat and leaned dangerously toward the water. Waving energetically, she called, "Hello! Andrea! Mario!"

Mario yelled back, "Sit down, darling! Don't stand in the boat!"

Mary Lousie, still standing, cupped her hands around her mouth. "*He* says we've stalled! We haven't been *any-where*."

At that moment, Kyle Hagen put the boat in gear. There was a jerking motion. Mary Louise lurched to the side. Francesca, now with both hands around the little girl's waist, lifted her back down into the seat.

Mario turned furiously to Tropard. "Good God! They're going to let her fall out of the boat before we even get there!"

"She's safe now." Tropard had the gun in his hand pointing it at Mario's rib cage. "Go ahead as we planned."

A shifting wind lifted water from the small boat's wake and sent a cold spray against Andrea's face and arms. She shivered and bent her head toward the bow.

A gondola glided toward them. Four women, wrapped in raincoats and wearing plastic scarves to protect their hairdos from the encroaching fog, smiled and called "*Buona sera!*" as they passed.

From the other side, a *vaporetto* approached filled with passengers bound for the hotels on the Lido.

From the distant maritime station, Andrea could hear a fog horn sounding a warning.

It was not a long boat ride—fifteen minutes at the most—to St. Mark's Square.

"Here. Turn in here," Tropard instructed. With his free hand he pointed to an empty slip just west of the granite pillar with the winged lion.

In the short time it had taken to get to the piazza, lights had been turned on in boats and on shore. There was enough remaining twilight so that the boats and the figures in them were still visible, though they appeared to be no more than silhouettes in varying dark shades of gray.

Mario cut the motor and made a sharp left turn—too sharp, and too fast. The boat scraped against the narrow wooden dock and hit, then bounced back from the buffer of rubber tires at the front.

Two gondoliers, who had been talking quietly nearby while they waited for a fare, looked with reproach at the small boat that had made such a clumsy landing.

Mario started to climb out the moment they were in the slip, but Tropard took hold of his arm.

"Monsieur Costantino, please do nothing else to call attention to us," he said sharply.

"I'm not used to a boat this size. I usually take the other one . . ."

"Whether it was your intention or not, I am warning you that we want no one to notice us. Hagen will be gone in a matter of seconds if anything untoward happens on shore. He will leave me stranded, and he will have your daughter with him. How he would choose to deal with her, I cannot say. Now, let's go to the vault and get this over with as quickly as possible."

Andrea and Mario both looked toward the *Villa Constance*. It was idling off shore: a distance the length of an Olympic swimming pool.

Tropard got out first and reached a hand down to Andrea. "I'm sure there's no need to remind you to bring your briefcase, Mademoiselle Perkins."

When she was standing on the dock, Tropard stepped aside and motioned for her to precede him. He waited for Mario, then took his arm guiding him in front by the elbow.

St. Mark's Square was less crowded than it had been earlier in the day. This was the hour when tourists were in their hotel rooms, changing for dinner, having cocktails or checking their itinerary for the following day. Some stragglers still sat talking and laughing at the outdoor tables. Others prevailed upon their friends to pose for flashbulb photographs. The orchestra, as usual, was on the bandstand, but was taking a break. The musicians smoked and joked quietly with the white-jacketed waiters who lounged against the pillars as they waited for the evening crowd. Most of the pigeons had gone to roost on the balustrades, balconies, ledges, and countless secret places where they huddled in the dark. A few of the heartier birds still pecked at crumbs around the feet of the tourists at the tables.

Low, unhurried conversation and laughter blended with the sound of lapping water. In the distance—somewhere on the Grand Canal—a gondolier sang "O Sole Mio."

When Mary Louise called out, probably no one but the three who had been in the small boat noticed.

Andrea, Mario, and Tropard had reached the end of the wooden dock and had stepped onto the concrete walkway.

"Mario!" The child's piping voice came to them across the water. "He says we have to stay here! I don't want to. I want to come with—"

Her words were cut off sharply by what was undoubtedly a hand clamped across her mouth.

Andrea and the two men turned to look toward the *Villa Constance*. Behind the driver was the outline of a little girl standing in the seat, struggling to get out of the arms of a veiled figure that stood behind her.

In that instant, Mario let go. The fragile control he had held on his emotions collapsed. He lurched at Tropard, swinging and grabbing at him.

"Don't do this, Costantino!" Tropard pulled away. "For the sake of your daughter!"

"*Polizia!*" Mario shouted at the two gondoliers. "This man is a criminal!"

The gondoliers watched without alarm. A fight at this end of the Grand Canal was not as common as it was nearer the maritime station, but it was not unknown.

Three tourists strolling toward the dock stopped short when they saw Mario swing.

Andrea stood frozen, not knowing what was the greater danger.

Mario yelled again. "*Polizia!*"

The tourists, not wanting to become involved, bypassed the two men and continued in the direction they had been going.

Tropard dodged away. Trying again to calm Mario he said, "She has not been harmed! Stop this!"

Mario leaped at Tropard. He knocked him to the concrete walkway. The momentum of the fall and their entangled legs spun them on their sides.

Until the moment they were on the ground, Tropard had tried to calm Costantino. Even as he scrambled to stand he said, "Costantino! Don't be a fool!"

But Mario's reason had been replaced by fury. He grabbed Tropard's coat as the Frenchman tried to stand, hooking his hand on the pocket and ripping down.

The gun clattered on the concrete between them. Tropard's hand touched it first. Mario's hand clamped over Tropard's. The gun was not aimed. The shot was not intended. It was not even clear who fired it. But the sound rang through the square and carried over the water.

Mario slouched to his knees. He clutched at his thigh. Throwing his head back he howled at the small crowd that had gathered. "Get help! My daughter's been kidnapped!"

The moment Mario released his grip, Tropard scrambled away, snatching the gun from the walkway. He saw there was no chance left to salvage his exquisite plan.

Plunging through a small group of teenagers who had been attracted by the noise but were unaware of the source, Tropard hurried toward a covered walkway on the piazza, confident that he could soon lose himself in the scattered crowd.

No one followed him. No one tried. The man who had been injured was yelling for the police and pointing toward a boat in the canal as though the shot had come from there.

It had all happened in less than a minute.

Andrea's concern from the beginning was with what would happen on the boat.

At the sound of the gun the motor on the *Villa Constance* started up.

The voice of Mary Louise rang above the sound of the sputtering motor. "Let me go!" For the first time she sounded afraid.

Hagen gunned the motor and turned the bow sharply. The boat tipped on its right side. The left side raised from the water. The sudden turn propelled Hagen to the center of the seat. He was forced to use his grip on the steering wheel to pull himself level again.

Mary Louise had been standing in the seat watching the struggle on shore. She had squirmed out of Francesca's grip. Francesca, momentarily off balance, stood behind the child then grabbed her by the shoulders to pull her back.

When the motor started and the boat made its radical turn, both Francesca and Mary Louise were jolted to the side. Holding only to each other, they had no way to resist the momentum and fell—over the side—into the canal.

Andrea saw it happen. She ran toward the boat on the narrow dock. She did not consciously jump into the water, but kept going toward the child even when the solid planks were no longer under her feet.

Mario had seen it, too, and tried to go after them, but his leg would not even hold him to stand.

"For God's sake, someone! Help them!"

The two gondoliers jumped in their gondolas. With expert maneuvering they glided into the canal, but their boats were not built for speed.

Someone ran down the walkway to find a police boat. Someone else sprinted to a public telephone in the square to call a rescue unit.

There was almost total darkness now. Andrea swam toward the churning water where the boat had been. At first she saw nothing. Then there was something white. A face framed in the white linen of the nun's habit broke the surface of the water. Francesca flailed at the water and made terrified gasping sounds.

"Where's the child—oh, God—where's the child!" Andrea swam toward where Francesca had been a moment before.

Suddenly, to her left—as yet out of reach—she saw a small blond head, facedown in the water.

In the time it took Andrea to take two more strokes, the head turned, the mouth opened to take in air, and the short arms and legs began to pummel the water like a small animal.

When Andrea reached her, she crooked one arm around the child's chest. "Keep your head up!"

Clumsily, she propelled them both toward shore. At the end of the dock, someone held a long narrow gondola pole out to her. She grabbed it with one hand. "There's someone else out there," she urgently told the small crowd that had gathered. "A girl in a nun's habit!"

With the child still firmly held in one arm, Andrea hung onto the pole, and let the man at the other end pull them through the water to the edge of the walkway.

She set the little girl down on a stone step and struggled up beside her.

Now, the canal seemed full of boats. The two gondolas

were there, a police boat—with siren blaring and lights sweeping across the water. A small private cruiser circled the area. And briefly, Andrea was sure she saw the *Villa Constance* return. It slowed and traversed the outer edge of the activity, then turned again in the direction of Connie Gilbert's villa.

A strong young man had helped Mario to his feet and held him at the waist with Mario's arm around his shoulder. Despite the urging of onlookers, Mario would not let them take him to the infirmary in the piazza. He would not move from the walkway until Andrea and Mary Louise were back on shore.

"*Grazie, grazie,*" Mario said over and over to Andrea, and with his free hand stroked the soggy curls on the little girl's head.

A rescue unit pulled into the slot vacated by one of the gondolas. Two attendants in white uniforms helped Mario onto a cot in the back of the boat. A nurse came on shore with blankets and draped one over Andrea's shoulders and wrapped Mary Louise in the other.

Andrea refused to go to the hospital with them. She was fine, she said. Her hotel was just across the square.

She bent down and hugged the shivering child. "You'll be all right, won't you?"

Teeth chattering, the little girl nodded. Then with serious blue eyes she looked up to Andrea and said, "I can swim by myself."

Andrea laughed and kissed her on the cheek.

Mary Louise giggled, but she did not seem to be sure of just why.

Andrea watched the rescue boat go, but still she did not leave. She stood back from the crowd that had gathered clutching the blanket around her. She knew Francesca was gone. It had been too long. She could not have survived. Finally, she turned to go to the hotel.

"Here! Over here!" one of the gondoliers shouted. "She's over here!"

Andrea ran back to the edge of the walkway as the searchlight from the police boat shone on the spot where the gondolier pointed.

Something white was just beneath the surface. With a net and a hook two policemen guided what they had found to the side of the hull.

The driver of the boat asked urgently, "Is it the nun?"

The man with the hook shook his head silently.

With the net, the second policeman pulled from the dark water a saturated black-and-white stuffed panda bear.

Andrea bunched the blanket around her as she pushed through the revolving door of the Hamilton Plaza. Water dripped from her clothes and the blanket onto the plush deep-red carpet.

A few people were chatting in the lobby. They all grew silent and turned to look when she entered. Andrea did not notice. The only person she saw was the tall man with black curly hair at the bank of guest telephones next to the reception desk.

Aldo Balzani slowly replaced the phone in the cradle and looked at her in stunned surprise when she wordlessly pulled at his sleeve. She stood beside him huddled and shivering in the damp blanket. Her shoes were gone and the gray dust that had clung to her feet as she crossed St. Mark's Square had become splotches of mud where the water had dripped. A small rivulet ran down beneath her chin as she tucked her wet hair behind one ear.

"Good Lord" was all he could manage to say. Putting out his arms he hugged her gently to him. She bent her head, resting the top of it against his chest. Her arms hung loose and she stared down at her dirty feet.

"I tried to call Mrs. Gilbert's villa," he said, "but there was no answer."

"No, there wouldn't have been," she said into his shirt front.

A sob or shiver or spasm shook her body. Balzani's arms tightened, pulling her so close she could feel a shirt button digging into her cheek bone.

He held her that way until she was breathing evenly. Then he put a hand under her chin and looked into her face. "I think at the very least," he said, "that you should put on shoes before we go to dinner."

When they were in her room he turned on the shower for her. She soaped and rinsed and stood in the hot steamy water until he knocked on the glass door. When she stepped out he wrapped her in her terry cloth robe and rubbed her wet hair with a big fluffy towel.

She told him part of what had happened, not in sequence, but in the order that was least painful.

Balzani ordered minestrone and bread and a large carafe of house red wine from room service. He propped the pillows against the head of the bed and they watched a videocassette of *Oklahoma!* as they ate.

Andrea was asleep before the movie was over. Her last waking thoughts as she threw an arm across Balzani's chest and found the spot where her head fit best beneath his chin were that she truly liked the Clorox smell of the sheets in the Hamilton Hotel chain, and that the Modigliani print on the wall was probably her favorite of all his paintings.

During the night, the attendant at the Piazzale Roma—the giant parking lot near the causeway—accepted payment for storage and gave a receipt to the owner of a black Porsche. The Porsche had been in the parking garage for some time, but the attendant remembered the distinguished-looking owner with white hair. He also remembered that there had been an attractive young brunette with him when he arrived. Ah, well. So were the fickle ways of young girls. He smiled and thought with rare appreciation of his own plump wife.

Early the next morning, while Andrea was still asleep, Balzani stood at the window looking down at the doorman sweeping the sidewalk. As Balzani watched, a group of tourists wearing badges came out through the revolving doors and assembled briefly in front of the hotel while a girl in a blue uniform gave them instructions. Then they all struck out together across St. Mark's Square. Walking beside the girl in the blue uniform was a young man in a corduroy jacket carrying a Bloomingdale's tote bag and a red, white, and blue umbrella.

Chapter Seventeen

It was two months later when Andrea returned to Venice.

She had meant to get back sooner, but restoration of a Carpaccio painting had kept her in Florence. The canvas had spent at least two of its more than four hundred years under a heavy coat of varnish that had to be painstakingly removed before the painting could be put on exhibition in the Galleria dell' Accademia.

Mario Costantino was waiting for her in the vault behind the Basilica when she arrived. He was on crutches but assured her that his leg was mending and that the bullet had caused no permanent damage.

As Andrea opened her briefcase and spread her notes on the wooden work table she asked, "How are Connie and Mary Louise?"

"Connie is fine." He shrugged and smiled. "Connie is always the same."

Mario turned away to pull a chair out from the table and

lowered himself into it, placing his crutches on the floor beside him. Without looking up he said, "And her granddaughter is also doing well. She is back in school at Pisa, but Connie plans to have her spend all next summer here."

So, Mary Louise is to remain only Connie Gilbert's granddaughter, Andrea thought. She said nothing, but reached out and closed her hand over Mario's for just a moment.

Mario cleared his throat and said, "They identified the body of that poor girl who drowned in the canal as someone from the Maggio Musicale in Florence."

"Yes, I know. The Florentine police had been looking for her."

"And Tropard and Hagen both managed to elude our Venetian police."

"Yes, so I understand."

"But at least they didn't manage to steal the Egyptian mask."

"No, at least they didn't get the mask."

Andrea took out several eight-by-ten photographs and placed them with her notes. "I took these that first day," she said.

They were shots from different angles of the bronze mask that was stored in a metal drawer there in the vault. "I know who he was," Andrea said.

Mario's expression was guarded. "You were able then," he asked, "to determine his age in your laboratory?"

"Yes. When the bronze was analyzed it turned out to be a mixture of tin and copper in the same proportions as the Egyptians used for sometime prior to and after the first century. Metal is not as easy to date as wood, however, so that was hardly conclusive. It was the wooden backing on the mask that convinced me." Smiling, she added, "That, and a three-year-old tourist's guide to Italy I brought with me when I came here from Boston."

"I'm sorry, I don't understand." Mario held his hands up in confusion.

"I ran a carbon-14 test on the sample of wood I took from the backing." Andrea handed Mario a photograph of the back view of the mask where a portion of the original wooden support remained. "I also analyzed a sample from that charred plank you showed me." She looked steadily at Mario. "I noticed that the wood from both was the same age."

Mario said nothing but continued to look at the photograph.

"You know who he was, too, don't you," Andrea said. It was not a question.

"There has never been proof."

Andrea handed him a frontal photograph. "This bronze Egyptian sculpture," she said softly, "is not a sculpture at all. It's a death mask of Saint Mark, isn't it?"

With a heavy sigh, Mario looked at the photographs one by one.

"That has to be the explanation." Excitement grew in Andrea's voice. "You told me that the plank—a plank from Saint Mark's casket—was all that protected the body when the Basilica burned. In the tenth century, I think it was."

"There has been more than one fire," Mario said. "But after the first disastrous experience, the church made sure the body was protected. That's why it's encased in granite now. Fire or flood will never harm it again."

Nor will it ever be analyzed, Andrea thought, but did not say.

"It was the fact that the mask was made in Egypt that confused me," Andrea continued, "until I read my guide-book. The book I have is H. V. Morton's *A Traveller in Italy*. But practically any guidebook in any bookstore has an account of how Saint Mark's body happened to be in Venice."

"Yes," Mario said, "it's our favorite bit of local history. Mark died in Alexandria, probably around ninety-six A.D. That was at a time and in a place where it was not safe to be a Christian." Mario grimaced as he shifted in his chair, rubbing his injured leg. "The Book of Mark was the first one actually written for the New Testament, you may or may not know. Before then, the story of Christ had been passed from group to group, from person to person by word of mouth. But the believers were becoming scattered, and persecution was becoming commonplace. And I suppose it was hard to remember spoken words when they were facing martyrdom. So Mark wrote his version of the story of Christ and had it smuggled around as a source of encouragement and strength for the Christian martyrs."

Andrea glanced down at a profile photograph of the mask, then turned her attention back to Mario.

"It was always known that his remains were in Alexandria," Mario continued. "And in the early ninth century—when Christianity had become popular—two Venetian sea captains arranged to smuggle the body out of Egypt to Venice. And Mark became our patron saint—the Lion of Venice."

"And the mask was in the casket with the body, wasn't it."

"There have always been stories that there was a death mask."

"But, Mario," Andrea said, "there is no mention of a mask in anything I have read. And yet the story of Saint Mark's body is included in practically every guidebook. The accounts vary from book to book, but they generally agree that the mummified body was hidden under a load of pork and cabbages so that the Moslems would not find it when it was smuggled aboard the ship."

"Yes, that's a simplified version."

Andrea stood and paced in front of the bank of locked metal drawers. "And then the Venetians were so pleased with themselves for pulling off this coup, that they built the Basilica—one of the most beautiful churches in the world—to honor Saint Mark. They commissioned mosaics and paintings and tapestries to proclaim to the world that Mark's body was the property of Venice. But the mask—the actual likeness of his face—is stored in a metal drawer in this vault next to the grisly remains of some obscure saints." She tapped with her fingernails at the drawer that held the mask. "Why?"

Mario shrugged. "I, like yourself, am concerned with the art of the church, not its religion."

"But what do you think the reason is?"

"It all began so long ago. Who can say who was responsible for making the decisions, or what the reasons were?"

Andrea persisted. "But what do you think?"

Mario's face grew flushed as though he were angry.

Andrea was surprised at his reaction. "I'm sorry," she said. "I didn't mean to press—"

"Look for yourself. Come here and look at this face."

Andrea took the full-face photograph of the bronze Egyptian mask from him and sat at the table again.

"Look at those eyes," Mario said. "Look at how demanding they are. No compromises, no excuses would be accepted by those eyes. And that ugly mouth. Whether it was distorted by death—or by life—it's so grotesque it makes you look away. That's a face to hide from, not kneel before."

Yes, Mario was right.

Connie had been right, too. Andrea remembered Connie's insistence that night at the villa that the Renaissance artists had equated physical beauty with spiritual beauty.

Thank heaven they had been inspired to create such

masterpieces, Andrea thought, even if the concept was not always true.

Mario pulled his crutches out from beneath the table. Holding on to the back of the chair, he stood, then balanced himself on the padded armrest. "I would like a cup of cappuccino," he said. "Let's go sit in the piazza in front of Florian's. I have a table permanently reserved in a place that offers the best view in Venice of our magnificent Basilica."

Epilogue:
California. Winter, a year later.

The limousine driver stopped in Crestline to put on snow chains. It had been awhile since he had driven a customer up here, but he remembered how treacherous the roads could be. Some of the wealthy people in San Bernardino who did not want to drive on this road themselves used to hire his limousine service fairly often. People used to come out here from Los Angeles, too. He wondered if they still did.

Cursing under his breath he got back into the driver's seat and headed onto the twisting road. That damned retreat was to hell-and-gone past the last ski lift on a ridge road that would scare a mountain goat. But then mountain goats had more sense than those religous nuts who lived at the retreat. At least goats had a healthy respect for rock slides and patchy ice.

Five miles past Snow Summit Lodge, the driver shifted into second and held his breath until he rounded the worst of the narrow curves. Thank God he did not meet one of the

Jeeps from the retreat coming around the bends. A Jeep was sure as hell what you needed if you were going to live in this godforsaken place.

At last the road curved away from the edge of the mountain and up a gravel slope toward a gate in a chain-link fence. When the limousine got within a hundred yards, the gate was opened by a boy of about eighteen or nineteen, the driver guessed. The boy wore a zipped-up parka and fur-lined gloves and pointed down the road toward a large single-story building with a satellite dish on its roof.

On each side of the road were dense pine trees, and scattered among them were neglected-looking A-frame cottages constructed of rough-hewn logs. Next to the central stucco building was a huge, fence-enclosed generator.

The building itself was one story of concrete brick and glass similar to those seen in industrial parks. Written in gold leaf on the glass slab on the front door was "Retreat in the Lord."

The driver parked in front.

"There's a snack bar in the back," the passenger told the driver. "I'll come tell you when I'm ready to leave." The man got out of the backseat and entered the building. He was wearing a corduroy jacket and carried a canvas bag.

The lobby was small. It was furnished with a well-used couch and several chairs grouped around a giant television set. A middle-aged woman in a pink velour warm-up suit looked up when the man entered. "Yes?"

"I'm Kyle Hagen," he said.

"Of course! Your father told me you were coming. He's in the studio, packing boxes, poor man. Just go right on through."

The recording studio was a jumble of packing crates, television cables, disassembled cameras, and lighting equipment. One man in coveralls had parts of a boom microphone in each hand. He carried them out to a loading platform when Kyle entered.

The Reverend Hagen, stacking video cassettes into a wooden box, nodded at his son but continued what he was doing. "You look the same," he said. "Ornery as ever."

"This place has gone to seed since I left," Kyle said.

"Too much competition on television these days. Too many places for people to send donations. It's time I retired, anyway."

"It's time I took over."

The Reverend Hagen's laugh was short and bitter. He squinted out the back door as the limousine pulled around. "Did you come up here in that?"

"Yeah. I want to get used to riding in one."

"You might be better off buying yourself a new jacket."

Kyle shrugged.

"I don't know what you've been up to, but we don't need a tour guide," his father said, "we need somebody who can pay the bills."

"What every church needs is a few special followers, isn't that what you always said? Just a few, who can put in enough heavy coin to make a deacon drop the collection plate."

"Do you know some?"

"You do—or used to."

"They've all wandered off in other directions."

"You could get them back if I started preaching."

The Reverend Hagen laughed again.

"You've got to have something special to attract them."

"And you think that's you?"

"It's what I've got in this bag."

Kyle Hagen put a canvas bag that said "Bloomingdale's" on its side in a chair next to his father. "I'm not going to tell you how I got this, and there's no need to tell anyone else, either."

He handed his father a sheet of vellum. The single sheet was decorated with an orante scroll around the edges. In script, at the top was written: *Galleria dell' Accademia, Florence, Italy.*

Someone had signed the document of authentication, *Andrea Perkins* on a line provided for that signature. A red wax seal with the face of a lion had been affixed beneath it. The text in the center described an object identified as: *The Death Mask of Saint Mark.*

"Holy God. What have you gotten ahold of, son?"

"Wait till you see."

Kyle Hagen reached into the Bloomingdale's bag again. With both hands he lifted an object wrapped in red velvet. He set it carefully on the floor in front of his father. What he unwrapped was a facial mask made of bronze. The face was bland . . . expressionless. Except that the eyes were closed, and the lips had been pulled into the mouth so that they disappeared and became a straight line, there was a marked resemblance between the mask and Kyle Hagen himself.

"We can't show this to everyone," he said excitedly, "because it didn't come through customs legally. The Italians have a law about taking objects of a certain age out of the country."

The Reverend Hagen stared at the mask, unable for the moment to comprehend what his son had shown him.

"They call Mark the Lion of Venice in Italy. But why should he belong only to the Venetians?"

"The first thing we need to do is change the name of this place to The Lion's Retreat. We may as well use the lion as our symbol . . ."

It was the hand of the Lion of Venice that wrote: "... *from within, out of the heart of men proceed evil thoughts, adulteries, fornications, murders, thefts, covetousness, wickedness, deceit, lasciviousness . . . blasphemy, pride, foolishness.*"